GET LUCKY

LUCKY IN LOVE #1

LILA MONROE

LILA MONROE BOOKS

ALSO BY LILA:

The Lucky in Love Series:

1. Get Lucky

2. Bet Me

3. Lovestruck

4. Mr Right Now

5. Perfect Match

6. Christmas with the Billionaire

Cupids Series (2019):

Cupids Anonymous

What's Your Sign?

The Romeo Effect

The Break-Up Artist

The Chick Flick Club Series:

1. How to Choose a Guy in 10 Days

2. You've Got Male

3. Frisky Business

Billionaire Bachelors Series:

1. Very Irresistible Playboy

2. Hot Daddy

3. Wild Card

4. Man Candy

5. Mr Casanova

6. Best Man

The Billionaire Bargain series

The Billionaire Game series

Billionaire with a Twist series

Rugged Billionaire

Snowed in with the Billionaire (holiday novella)

1

JULIA

WAKING up in Vegas was always a treat. But for Lola Sinclair, industrial saboteur and sexual adventurer, waking up with a rock-hard arm around her stomach and a rising erection against her back was the only way to start the day in Sin City. She was still lingering in the delicious aftereffects of a dream as his fingers trailed down her stomach to flit gently across her pussy.

Hmm. Flit gently. Not sure it's the best word choice, but whatever. I can always edit later.

Lola smiled, her lips parting as Archer rolled his thumb around her clit. His finger pushed inside of her, and she was instantly wet. Hopefully, his rock-hard cock would soon follow.

Yeah. That's good. Maybe we could have something more descriptive, like a simile? "She was instantly wet, like a St. Tropez beach at high tide."

Eh, maybe not.

Lola groaned deep in her throat as he fingered her, his other hand tracing delicate patterns across her naked back. "Damn," she thought, *"I am going to hate to wake up from this dream. I—"*

Wait a minute.

My eyes snap open. Lola Sinclair's not the one in Vegas; I am. She's not the one with someone waking her by saying good morning to her clit; I am. Lola Sinclair, BDSM sexpert and awesome international spy, doesn't even exist; I just write books about her. And it's not Archer Valmont, sadistic billionaire and champion badminton player, with his rock-hard arm around my stomach and his rising erection flush against my . . . .

What the flying fuck? Who the hell am I in bed with?

I turn to find a stubbled, ruggedly handsome face on the other pillow. The man wakes up slowly, bedroom eyes dreamy. His dark hair is tousled from what must have been an athletic night. The smile stretched across his face slowly collapses as he takes me in, and his eyes widen with shock.

Oh God. Where the fuck am I, and who the fuck is this?

"What the hell?" the mystery man grunts.

I try to roll away from him, but I'm too tangled in the sheets.

So, tangled and rolling, I fall out of bed and hit the floor.

2

NATE

LOGIC IS MY FRIEND.

Whenever I'm on the phone with a client, guiding him or her through the trauma of a contentious divorce, I remember I'm supposed to be the one with the level head and the ironclad plan. Whenever people sit across from me, blubbing into a packet of Kleenex while going on about how it's over, how *can* it be over, I'm the man with a pitcher of ice cold drinking water and a detailed list of why they should be fucking *glad* it's over. *He cheated on you. She's looking to take full custody and half your annual salary. Why would you want to put yourself through this hell one more day?* Calm, orderly thoughts lead to calm, orderly lives. No surprises means no surprising fuck-ups.

So when I wake up slowly from a dream about having a round, sexy ass pressed up against my morning wood, I'm happy to languish. What man wouldn't? It'd felt so real.

Turns out it felt real because it *was* real. And when I snap back to consciousness and find myself face to face with a pair of enormous blue eyes and a tangled mane of strawberry blonde hair, I realize I don't know where the hell I am or who the hell I'm with.

Focus, Nate. And do it fast, because she looks like she's about to start screaming.

First part comes back easy. I'm in the Bellagio hotel, Las Vegas, in a damn sweet, well, suite. Top floor, corner penthouse, killer view of the Strip at night. No, I'm not rolling in money, though I'm certainly not hurting for cash. I've guided enough high profile billionaires through painless divorce settlements that it gets me a few perks. Like free Vegas hotels whenever I feel like it.

Okay. We're in the hotel. That's clear to me.

But the strawberry blonde with the increasingly terrified blue eyes? That one's not so clear. And I don't like it when I don't know the answer to a very important question.

So take it easy, Nate. Proceed with caution. Maybe start with—

"What the hell?"

Okay, not the most eloquent, but can you fucking blame me?

The woman twists around and falls off the bed. Shit. I sit up at once and discover that I'm completely naked. Great. So is she.

"Are you okay?" I ask, leaning over the bed. She looks up at me, blinking herself awake, and pushes her curls out of her face.

"What am I doing here?" she snaps, clutching the sheets to cover her (ample) breasts as she gets up off the floor. Which leads to question three.

"Why are you naked?" I say.

"Why are *you* naked?"

"It's my bed." *Yes!* Pwned by logic. I'm doing pretty good so far, considering my erection is still at half mast.

I rub my eyes and fish around for my pants. Where the fuck *are* my pants? I spot them flung across the room, decorating the lampshade. My aim last night was either awesome or for shit.

"Okay, hold on. I remember you," I grumble, running a hand through my hair. It's coming back to me, slowly and in a blur. I snap my fingers. "Jenny!"

"Julia," she corrects. She sighs, loses her sense of modesty, and drops the sheet. And as freaked out as I am right now, I appreciate the view.

She runs around the room collecting her clothes. What do I do? Look away, not look away? What's the best option here? I think I should avert my eyes, though when she bends over, I find it hard to tear my gaze away from that that fantastic ass. Hell, I'm only human. And there's something drawing my attention—oh shit. My eyebrows shoot up.

"You got a tattoo," I say.

"Huh?" She cranes her neck to look over her shoulder, but she can't glimpse what I'm seeing: a weird looking blue box, planted right on the small of her back.

"What is that thing?" I ask as she runs to the closet door mirror and turns around.

She sees it now, and curses. The ink looks fresh, and there's a plastic wrap pasted to her skin that's halfway falling off. She must've gotten it last night. I can't help grinning. People make shitty choices in Vegas.

"I did it. I actually got the TARDIS on my ass," she whispers, looking horrified.

Tortoise? What?

"A TARD-ASS, if you will." She giggles a little. Then the woman—Julia—stops and looks at me quizzically. "Wait. Get up and turn around."

My smile evaporates. *Oh, shit.* I wondered what that tingling feeling on my lower back was. I get out of bed—treating her to a full show—and check myself in the bathroom door's mirror.

Fuck me. Some weird black symbol, right above my ass.

"What is it?" I grunt. "Chinese?"

She scoffs at my ignorance. "No, doofus. It's the rebel alliance symbol from *Star Wars.*"

Holy shit. I've been branded a nerd.

Okay, keep calm. You can still make partner with this. At least it's not on your forehead. Oh my God.

"What the hell did we do last night?" I say.

Be calm. I need to be calm right now, because Julia seems to be starting to hyperventilate with laughter at my tattoo. God, that's annoying.

There it is, a twinge of recognition—this woman annoys me.

"You want to knock it off?" I say. She puts her hands up and gets herself under control.

"Okay, last night. All I know is there were shots. Shots everywhere. On everything." She groans and rubs her face. "Probably mostly tequila. My mouth tastes like a whorehouse in Tijuana. Speaking of, do you have any more shots?"

"Of what?" I grunt. She shrugs in response.

"Of booze? I think a little hair of the dog would help right now. Or maybe the whole damn dog." She blinks and screws up her face. "I've had some hangovers in my time, but Jesus."

She's not wrong. My own head feels like someone's pounding to be let out. Like they left their keys outside my skull, and they need to get them right the fuck now.

"Check the kitchen. There should be a bottle of champagne at all times. Like I ordered." I take a deep breath. This is fine. Mostly. I'm just naked with a stranger, sporting an ass tattoo, and my maybe-probably hook-up is a morning drinker.

Vegas does shitty things to you.

"Ooh, constant champagne? Fancy. Dom Perignon? I don't settle for anything else." She bats her eyelashes at me, over-the-top flirtatious.

And I can't help it. I laugh. And that gives me a fucking migraine.

"If I were you, I'd settle for a cup of coffee and some Excedrin," I say, rubbing my head.

"Breakfast of champions. Do you always treat your dates this way?" she drawls, finally wriggling into her black lace panties. I try not to watch that little dance, because my cock is perking up and I don't need this right now.

"You're not my date." I think my skull is about to start melting. I haven't been hungover like this since sophomore year.

She juts her chin out. "You know, you are definitely the type of guy to completely fuck up an easy score. I mean, a naked woman in your bed? Most guys would be turning on the charm like—" Then she snaps her fingers, a wild light in her eyes. "I got it! Nate! That's your name."

"You win the door prize." I grab my pants from off the lamp.

I can't help but notice that Julia's eyes track down my body. She thoughtfully bites her lip—maybe she likes what she sees. I'm a little tempted to turn around, give her a full frontal show. Again, my cock's at the ready. *Fucking stop it, dude.* But curvy redheads were always one of my weaknesses. Even when they're insulting me.

"So. We both must have been crazy bombed last night, right?" Julia says. Her cheeks tinge pink. "Because I'm not really the type of person to wake up all *The Lost Weekend*, you know?"

"Don't worry about it. As far as either of us is concerned, this never happened." Whatever *did* happen, that is. I kind of want to ask if she remembers, but I also don't really want to find out.

"Fine. Great."

Is she being short with me? Was my response not flattering enough for her?

"Well, as they say in old Hollywood, don't call us. We'll lose your number and pretend you never existed," she says.

"They didn't say that. Did I give you my number?" I grab my phone and flip through the contacts, but nope. Nothing.

Julia rolls her eyes. "Relax, O Anxious One. You shall remain unmolested. At least, you won't be molested further." She wrinkles her nose. "Now if you'll excuse me, I'm off to the Grey Havens."

She pulls her shirt on over her purple lacy bra. I'm a little sad to see that go, even as I want to get her out the door.

"Grey Havens. Is that the hotel café?" I ask.

She starts laughing hysterically. She has to lean against the wall, her face flushing pink with exertion. Apparently I'm amusing.

"Oh, I needed that. Humor keeps us all from going insane, you know? See you around, Nate." She blows an air kiss, and then slips into some impractically tall heels.

We head to the front door, and she spins around, striking a dramatic pose. "Tell me you'll never forget me," she says, her head tilted back and one hand flung into the air.

"Bye," I say, ushering her out and closing the door after her.

I lean my forehead against that door for a second, taking a deep breath. *All right. Calm. Under control.* First I need to head for the bathroom, to shower and clean off the smell of cheap booze and sweat.

There's a knock at the door. Shit, she probably forgot something. I open up to find a valet holding an extraordinary bouquet of flowers. And when I say extraordinary, I mean tacky beyond all reason. Brightly colored roses, explosions of baby's breath, pink and orange tiger lilies sprayed with glitter and rearing up out of the back of the arrangement. There are even miniature blown-glass flowers, bright yellow and neon blue. I rub my eyes and shake my head.

"The wedding venue's the pavilion. Take it down—"

"Wedding?" The valet blinks at me. Maybe if I close the door on him, it'll send a message.

"Yeah, Kaufman-Rosenbaum wedding."

"Nate Wexler?" the kid asks. Oh, fuck. "Delivery. You ordered these last night."

Of course I did. I stare at the monstrous bouquet, wanting to punch it in its flowery face. "You don't remember any other spectacularly ridiculous things I did last night, do you?" I grumble as I stand aside and let him in. The valet trots into the living room and deposits the bouquet on the coffee table. He blinks again, a hotel-employed deer in the headlights.

"I just deliver flowers," he mumbles. I grab my wallet, tip him, and he leaves while I stare at the gargantuan floral display. There's a card, at least. I grab it and read it.

Julia,

I can't believe we did that. You're so fucking sexy.

I actually ordered a floral arrangement and had the florist put *that* on the card. But that's not even the worst part. "I can't believe we did that"? Well, what the flying fuck did we do?

As I stumble into the bathroom, turn on the shower and get in, my mind races. Did we actually fuck? Where did we go last night, and what did we do? Will this pounding headache ever go away?

When the hell did I get a tattoo?

What did we do that I couldn't believe?

Seriously. What the fuck happened yesterday?

3

NATE

"NATE THE GREAT! My man, how are you?" Tyler Berkley lifts his Ray-Bans and gives me a huge high five as I walk into the lobby. My high five is more sedate than his. But as Albert Schweitzer once said, you don't leave a brother hanging.

"I'm doing good, apart from still being hounded by a nickname that should've died ten years ago," I say, though I clap Tyler on the shoulder. For Tyler, ten years is no time at all. I've long since traded in my stained college tees for a professional suit and tie. Meanwhile, Tyler's still wearing board shorts and a tank top, like it's senior year. Even flip flops, God help us all. Some things don't get old. At least, not to Tyler Berkley.

"Where's the party?" I ask, peering around the bustling lobby. The place is expansive, cream and gold, with enormous and colorful blown glass flowers decorating a section of the ceiling. The marble floors are polished and buffed to perfection.

"Party's right this way, my man," Tyler says with a

grin. He puts his fingers in his mouth and whistles loudly. A couple of perfect ten girls in sundresses walk by, eyeing us with disdain.

Not like Tyler notices. "Hey! Nate's on deck!" he calls through cupped hands, making this process as embarrassing as possible. He then starts whooping, and I sigh as I roll my suitcase over to meet the wedding party. Tyler may be a man in his early thirties, but age would never matter to him.

Already, I can see Mike, the groom himself, talking to the lady at the reception desk. I try to steer myself around a cluster of people standing right in the center of the lobby. They've got that dazed, touristy look about them.

"Whoa!" A woman bolts around the herd of people, runs smack into me, and almost sends me to the ground. I manage to stay upright, but she's not so lucky. She tumbles to the floor, her bag tipping over and the plastic handle making a loud smacking sound. I hold out a hand to help her up—I know I'm kind of a dick, but I hope I'm not an asshole.

Still, even with this gallant gesture, I can't help judging the bag itself. It's shiny and purple. I prefer a more sedate color palette.

"Thanks," she says, taking my hand and pulling herself to her feet. Her smile is wide and bright, like crashing into people on a regular basis is just her way of saying hello. "Man, is it hopping or what?" She laughs, pulling her purse up onto her shoulder. Her laugh is kind of charming, actually. And even though I'm questioning her taste in luggage, I also find myself taking her in.

She's short and curvy, her strawberry blonde hair flyaway. She's got big blue eyes and a genuinely warm smile. Cute and approachable. Normally I'd be tempted to keep talking to her. But right now, I've got this bachelor party to deal with.

"You shouldn't run around like that," I tell her, and glance over at Mike. He's waving, giving a puzzled shrug. The woman huffs.

"Thanks, Dad," she mutters. Rolling her eyes, she, well, rolls away, her suitcase traveling behind her.

There she goes. It probably wouldn't have amounted to much, anyway. I tend not to do well with women who are into shiny things. They're the kind of people who like crocheting and cats. And crocheting things for their cats.

Finally, I finish my journey across the lobby and join Mike and Tyler.

"Vegas, baby!" Tyler yells, pumping his fist in the air.

Here we go—another *Swingers* line. I swear, I think that movie is Tyler's bible.

"Don't look at me like that, Wexler," he says, jabbing his finger in my face. "You want the strippers and booze as much as I do, man."

"I'm pretty sure you outdo me in that department," I tell him. Tyler just laughs.

"Rough flight?" Mike asks, pulling me into a quick hug and slapping me on the back. "Or just being your usual charming self?"

"Sorry, guys. Probably just tired. Where's Stacy?"

Mike's fiancée is here as well, with her own bachelorette party in tow. Much as I'd like to warn him off marriage—it's a dying institution, one that worked when it was designed for combining lands and trading cattle—I have to admire his choice of wife. Then again, it shouldn't surprise me. Even in our Northwestern days, Mike was always into the smart, sexy type. So was I, for that matter. But I don't have a type anymore. It's safer this way.

"She and the girls are checking out the casino," Mike says, grinning.

"Slots, right?" Tyler guffaws like he made a dirty joke.

"No, blackjack. Stacy'll probably clean them out."

"And then we'll be in trouble with hotel management." I finally get to the registration desk. The woman behind it has perfect hair and a perfect smile. "The tables are all rigged," I say. "Did you ever hear of Jeffrey Ma? He was an MIT student, learned how to count cards—"

"Nate. Dude. Not this weekend, okay?" Mike says, clapping me on the shoulder. "This is about love, man. Not numbers."

Mike's a good guy. There's no reason he should still be friends with a dick like me. But I won't lie; I'm glad that he is.

"Check it out," Tyler says, nudging me right in the ribs. "Ladies off the port bow."

I look over to the tanned girls in sundresses who had rolled their eyes at us earlier. They continue rolling their eyes as Tyler whoops and asks them to come over.

Mike shakes his head, and I sigh.

"Maybe we can hang with them later. Set you up good, man," Tyler says, punching me in the arm. Hell, maybe I do need to lighten up. It's Mike and Stacy's wedding, after all, not mine.

Not my wedding. That thought slips past my protective barriers to punch me right in the gut. I know why I'm in such an especially shitty mood right now, and it has nothing to do with women running into me, or Tyler hitting on everything in sight.

It's the wedding itself. It's who I don't have at my side. Not anymore.

Well, fuck it. This is Mike and Stacy's big celebration, and I'm not going to wreck it for them. I won't let myself be that weak.

The girl behind the desk slides me a paper envelope containing my keys. "Enjoy your stay, sir. Welcome to the Bellagio," she says, smiling.

"Thanks," I say. I even force a smile of my own. Who knows? I do it enough, maybe the smile will eventually become real.

4

JULIA

THE ROMANTIC STYLE convention is the one I look forward to every single year. I mean, how could I not? A full weekend of panels, piña coladas, and fabulous talk with romance-hungry readers? Sign me up. And the fact that it's in Vegas, capital of good times and steak for under five dollars, only makes it more alluring. I'm always ready for every party, with my heels on and my makeup on point. I love my readers, I love my fellow authors, and I love love. Which, being a romance novelist, I probably should.

The fact that it's being held at the Bellagio Hotel this year is icing on a delicious, buttercream cake. *Ocean's 11*! Sabotage! Breaking into things! Hot people! Not that I'll be doing any of those things, but I'm in close proximity to the people who do them! Yay!

But there's always the pesky matter of being on time. And I confess that I'm not great at that. Like, for instance, right now. I have to meet my agent in the bar for a drink.

"Gangway! Coming through," I say, hustling through

the crowd, and bam. I smack into someone tall, dark, and rumpled looking. I tumble to the floor, and my bag goes flopping with me. *No!* Damn, I hope the fall didn't wreck my crochet patterns. There's a tea cozy I'm having a particularly difficult time with right now.

Fortunately, the dude is a gentleman, and helps me up.

"Man, is it hopping or what?" I laugh as I look up into his face. Then I almost choke on my words, because dreamy guy is dreamy.

His eyes are a flashing dark blue, his jaw square and impeccably shaved, his dark brown hair combed back neatly. He's wearing a slightly rumpled business suit— probably came in first class from New York or London. I instantly start using his panty-dropping good looks as a template for my next romantic hero. Clive Razor, a sadistic billionaire who gets what he wants. That is, until a certain tenacious young woman enters his life, masquerading as his newest squash partner—

"You shouldn't run around like that," the dreamy guy says, sounding pissed. His handsome features collapse in a judgmental frown. And just like that, the romantic bubble pops. I don't need dream visions of surly jerks in my life. I have enough of those in reality.

Damn. I was maybe gonna masturbate to him later. That dream is dead now.

"Thanks, Dad," I mutter, grab my bag, and take off. Well, that was a disappointing run-in. But it doesn't matter. I've got my key, and now I've just got to get to the bar. I can drop my stuff off in the room later—the one I'm sharing with Shanna.

There it is—the Baccarat bar. It's right off the casino floor, modern style gray couches and chairs centered around low polished tables, a spray of blue blown glass flowers erupting out of the middle of the carpeted area. The vases of flowers and grand piano kind of contrast with the action and energy out on the gambling floor, but I think it's great.

Some people hate Vegas, with all its flashing lights and high volume slots. Me, I love the energy.

I spy Shanna already. It's hard to miss her, with her hair dyed bright blue and the sleeve tattoo of Japanese flowers on her right arm. She's talking with . . . yep. That's my agent.

"Who do I have to fuck to get served around here?" Meredith yells, holding up her now-empty Moscow Mule cup and waving it around. Meredith Chambers, hottest romance agent in New York, filthiest mouth east of the Mississippi. Or west, come to think of it. Some women walking by give her a shocked, slightly annoyed expression. She responds with aplomb. "Legs together, ladies. I'm not afraid of a little muff diving."

"I'm pretty sure you can get sued," I tell her, walking up to them.

Shanna beams and gives me a hug, and Meredith cackles, full on throwing her head back. She's still dressed to the nines; I never see her in anything less than a Chanel pantsuit. Flashing the Rolex watch on her wrist, gold jewelry jangling, she checks the time. She looks all of her fifty-seven years, and she makes them look good.

Meredith keeps snapping her fingers until, finally, a nervous looking waiter comes over.

"May I get you another?" he squeaks.

"Mule or orgasm?" she asks, eyeing him up and down, sizing him up. I think he's going to melt in fear.

All right, is this bordering on sexual harassment? Maybe. But the occasional double standard does wonders for women.

Meredith hands off her cup, and I sit. "There's my gorgeous fucking rock star. Look, you didn't hear this from me," she says, looking around in an exaggerated manner, "but *Forbidden Desire* is coming out on the *Times* list. You can get on Twitter in about an hour. Number five."

"Number five?" I gape, incredulous and exhilarated. Shanna hugs me again, and we almost fall over. But damn, does it matter? *The New York Times* list.

"This calls for more prosecco," Shanna says, pouring some.

Aw, she got a bottle and an extra glass, just for me.

"You spoil me," I say, toasting her.

"Best friend burden. Besides, we have more than one thing to celebrate today." She gives me an encouraging smile. "You must be happy, Jules."

Oh. Right. That. "Thanks," I murmur.

"What happened? You fucked the cabana boy?" Meredith asks, scrolling through emails on her phone.

"No. My divorce is final," I say, trying to sound cheery. And I do. Mostly. Even Meredith stills for a minute. Wow, she actually looks sort of chastened.

"Sorry, kid. I have a huge fucking mouth." She squeezes my hand. "Congratulations. I know what a prick he was."

This is the part where I should shout "hell fucking yeah" and jump up, fist in the air, superhero style. Then we would all whirl around and turn into a bunch of bright spandex-suited ladies and run off to fight marvelous amounts of crime and eat copious amounts of cake.

But instead, I force a smile and nod. I had been married to Drew for five years. He had been a delight for four of them. Then my career had taken off, and so had he.

"Hey," Shanna says, gently nudging me out of my funk. "Want to wave those guys over?" She points to three men walking along the casino floor. One of them's rolling a bag. *I feel that burden, brother.* "Three of them. One for each of us." She winks, and Meredith guffaws.

"I'm old enough to be their mother," Meredith says. "So I would definitely fuck them. Let's do this." She whistles and waves at the masculine trio. One of them looks nice and, basically, normal. The other has a gelled hair, Axe body-sprayed, pleasant doofus look about him. And the third, with the rolling suitcase, he's . . . .

Shit. It's tall, dark and scowling. He surveys us with a clearly bored and sullen expression.

"What's wrong? You look like you swallowed a Nuva-Ring," Shanna says, looking alarmed.

"I'm fine," I say quickly, and dammit, I mean it. Fuck it. I came here to drink a lot, laugh a lot, and gamble in moderation. Mr. Tightass can't spoil my good time.

"Ladies," Axe Bodyspray says, sliding over to us. He whips off his sunglasses; why the hell was he wearing them indoors? "Mind if we join you for an appetizer?"

"Apertif?" Shanna says, though she laughs. "I think that's what you meant."

To this guy's credit, he doesn't get flustered or douchey. He laughs right along. Hey, if there's one thing I appreciate, it's a good sport.

"Sounds good. Let's get together and make some magic happen." God, that line. He's kind of adorable in a frisky puppy sort of way.

Axe Bodyspray takes a seat between Meredith and Shanna. The normal guy sits a little farther away, smiling at all of us but not leaning in. I get the feeling he's taken. And that leaves only the seat next to me available for Tightass.

"Hello," the jerk says, blandly and pleasantly. He looks like we're meeting for the first time.

Great, I must've made an indelible impression when I smacked into him in the lobby and fell over. He doesn't remember three minutes ago. Which is fine. I totally don't want to remember it either. Even if he's got those Clive Razor godlike looks.

"What are you boys doing here?" Meredith asks, leaning back to scope out Axe's ass. He doesn't seem to be put off by it.

"Bachelor party. For me," normal guy says with a smile.

There you go. My romantic instincts are never wrong.

"Who's the lucky lady? Or guy?" Shanna asks.

"Lady. My fiancée, Stacy. She's around here some-where. Name's Mike Rosenbaum." He shakes with us. "That's Tyler Berkley," he says, pointing to Axe, "and Nate Wexler."

That would be Tightass McGee right here.

"Julia Stevens," I say, holding out my hand to him, my eyebrow arching. "We bumped into each other back at check in."

"I remember," he says, giving my hand a quick, firm

shake. "I remember that." He eyes my suitcase with something like disgust.

Wow. Not talking to this dick any longer. I smile over
at Mike instead.

"What are you gorgeous ladies doing all alone in
Vegas?" Tyler asks, wiggling his eyebrows at Shanna.

"We're at the Romantic Style convention. It lasts the
whole weekend," Shanna says, sipping her drink.

"You're romance writers?" Mike asks with a smile. He
seems genuinely interested. "That's crazy. My fiancée is
obsessed, maybe she's heard of you."

"I write under A.M Leroy," Shanna says. "It wouldn't
surprise me if she hasn't heard of my books, though.
They're a little—er—out there. Kind of have a niche
audience."

Shanna always sells herself short. "What she means is
she writes sci-fi erotica with amazing world-building and
really kinky sex," I say. "Android bondage? Bisexual alien
queens with a harem? That right there is your lady."

Shanna blushes a little. "Julia's the bestseller," she
says, grinning. "And she actually writes under her own
name. That's kind of rare in our profession."

"So I can actually find Julia Stevens at the bookstore?"
Mike says. "I like that."

"Just seemed like the honest thing to do," I say with a
laugh and a shrug.

"Honest?" Nate says. And there he goes. Tightass
McGee makes a harrumphing noise deep in his throat. If I
were a little more polite, and hadn't just had a glass or
two of fabulous afternoon prosecco, I might let this one
go. But I'm not, and I have, so I won't.

"Got a problem with your throat? Lozenge?" I ask, smiling sweetly. "Need some hot tea with honey?"

I'm not letting it go gracefully. Nate sighs.

"I don't mean to be rude," he says, his deep, rich voice going deeper and richer with condescension. *Such* condescension. Oh, do me now. "I just think the whole romance thing leads to unrealistic expectations. Expectations that do harm down the line."

He reclines slightly in his chair, gorgeously imperious. If Mr. Darcy was a modern man with a rolling suitcase, a stick shoved way up his ass, and no actual redeemable qualities, he might be this guy.

Now everyone's kind of stewing in awkwardness, and my blood is boiling. Mike clears his throat, obviously telling Nate to shut the hell up.

"Well, what line of work are you in?" I say, crossing my arms.

"Divorce attorney," he replies, his tone effortless and cool. His gaze locks with mine, his eyes the deep blue of a perfect midnight sea filled with fucking nasty sharks. "Too many couples come into my office because they're *incompatible*. Normally, you do a little digging and find it's a lot of dissatisfaction on the wife's part." He adopts a slightly higher tone of voice. It's a little whiny, too. " 'He's not spontaneous. He's not enthralling. He doesn't go down on me enough.' "

Nate raises his hand, and a waiter instantly appears. Doesn't surprise me that he's the kind of guy people instinctively know to serve right away. Nate orders three scotches on the rocks—imagine that, ordering for his friends—and the waiter's off like a shot. Nate Tightass is clearly used to getting his own way. And he is pissing me right the fuck off.

"So you blame marital issues on the romance industry?" I say, digging my nails into my thigh. Legally, it beats sinking them into his perfect, arrogant throat. Though it's not nearly as satisfying.

Nate shrugs. "I blame it on society selling women— and men, to be fair—a bill of goods. Men, we've got the *Sports Illustrated* swimwear issue and porn to get us started down the path to inevitable disappointment. With women, it starts even earlier, in infancy. You know. Disney princesses and all that other horseshit."

Horseshit? Fuck you. I will defend my Belle and Mulan awesome warrior princess road comedy fan fiction to the fucking death.

"So what you're saying is that love, chemistry, mutual happiness, it's all a huge fucking farce?" Meredith says, her voice so flat it could be mistaken for a county in Nebraska.

Tyler is staring at all of us with his mouth slightly open. Clearly, he doesn't know what to say.

"I should be grateful. If people didn't swallow the wrong messages, the wrong ideas about lasting love, I'd be out of a job," Nate says, staring me right in the eyes. "How about you, Ms. Stevens? Found your happy ending yet?"

I could lie to him. But before I think to do anything that smart, I tell the truth.

"I'm divorced." I swallow after I say it. No matter how many times I speak the words, think them, it's still a gut punch.

"I see," he says, no emotion in his voice. His dark blue

eyes seem to sparkle with gleeful light. "Too bad you didn't come to me. I could've gotten you a hell of a settlement."

My life is in tatters, and this asshole is making jokes about it. Apparently even his friends think this is over the line.

"Nate, what the fuck?" Mike says. His eyes are flashing, angry. The normal one has had enough. "The fuck is wrong with you, man?"

And for the first time, I see Nate the Tightass freeze and look regretful. Not because of me, probably, but he's basically pissing on the idea of lasting love at his friend's goddamn bachelor party. Nate clears his throat.

"I'm only saying what my experience has been," he says at last, though maybe with the tiniest hint of remorse.

And I could be the grown-up here, get up and walk away all nice and quiet. But lucky me, the booze arrives just as I've reached my limit. Three scotch on the rocks. Before he can take the glasses, I grab one tumbler.

"Experience this," I say, dumping the expensive contents on his shirt. He jumps like a very alcoholic spider just bit him. I slam the glass down, grab my trusty purple suitcase, and roll away at high speed.

Blood's pounding in my temples, and the edges of my vision are blurring with tears.

Calm down. Be one with the Force. Use every Jedi mind trick you know.

"Hey," Shanna gasps, rushing up beside me. I slow down. Just a bit. "That got really intense, huh?" Her eyes widen. I sigh.

"Sorry. It's been kind of a weird month."

" 'Experience this.' I fucking love it. What a line,"

Meredith says, waltzing up beside me. She puts an arm around my shoulders. "Think of it this way, hon. This is a big city, big enough to lose even the smuggest of assholes. Feel better."

"Thanks," I mutter, hugging her in return. She's got a point. One nice thing is the hotel is huge and the convention is busy. I never have to see that jackass again.

5

JULIA

I CAN'T BELIEVE I slept with that jackass. What is *wrong* with me?

All right, don't panic Julia.

Frazzled, I take the elevator down to ten and hustle back to my room. The plastic key card slips out of my hands once, twice, until finally I get the door open and stumble inside. I walk into the bedroom, grateful for the fact that at least the curtains are still drawn. The room exists in that cozy almost twilight, Shanna's bed still rumpled from having been slept in. Mine, on the other hand, is pristine, the sheets perfect, the pillows plumped. Never made it back here last night.

Oh God. Think, Julia. Did you actually do the nasty? Did you fuck the Worst Guy Ever? And if you did, can you remember if he was good or not?

Wow, brain. Not the time.

I groan as I flip on the lights and rush into the bathroom. I need a shower. That's it. A good hot shower will stop the pounding headache. I look at the mirror over the sink, grimacing at my smeared eye makeup. Then, just to make sure, I pull down my skirt, turn around, and bam. Tattooed TARDIS, right square over my ass. My Whovian heart has led me astray at last.

"Well, Ten, here's another fine mess you've gotten us into," I grumble.

Confession: I like to imagine that the Tenth Doctor is kind of like the physical embodiment of my wild and crazy side. I mean, he's played by David Tennant. How could he not be reckless?

Okay, I need to focus on things other than my imaginary Time Lord and my hangover. I groan and close my eyes. This is all alcohol's fault. God as my witness, I will never do shots again. For at least forty-eight hours, that is.

I turn on the shower full blast. I'm pretty sure this is going to mess with my tattoo—I try smoothing the square of plastic wrap back over it—but fuck it. There is no time. Before I get in the stall, I look back at my reflection. I need a pep talk.

"Okay, stay calm," I say aloud, my voice a little jarring in the otherwise silent hotel room. I breathe deeply. Nothing terrible has happened. It's not like I'm late for any—

Oh fuck. I rush into the bedroom to check the clock on the nightstand, and freak out a little. Shit. My panel! *Sex, Lies, and Superspies* starts in half an hour!

"Shitballs and fucksticks," I mutter, and run out to the bed to grab my laptop. And that's when I make a wonderful, nauseating discovery: my purse and laptop aren't here. At all. Even when I get on my hands and knees and inspect under the beds, under the table, and in every cabinet drawer, they still elude me. I plant my face in a pillow and give a loud, muffled scream.

Okay, Julia. Don't melt down. Don't go on a rampage. Think. And maybe shower, because you smell like cigarettes and bad decisions.

I rush back to the bathroom, undress fully, yanking off my bra and panties, and jump into the shower. I lather up as fast as I can. I'm out, toweled, and dressed in ten minutes flat. My makeup is hastily applied in an additional three.

Okay. I stand back and admire myself in the mirror. Cute. I look cute. It looks a little bit like I made out with the Joker and took off some of his lipstick, but right now there's nothing much else I can do.

"Nate Wexler. You are a monster," I grunt. Then I grab my key and race out the door. *Damn, damn.* I'm supposed to be at my panel at least ten minutes beforehand. This is cutting it dangerously close.

I race down the carpeted halls, take the elevator, and soon find myself standing outside one of the galleria rooms. There are clusters of women chatting together as I stumble towards the raised stage. A woman with a clipboard and a tense expression rolls her eyes as I stagger up to her.

"Sorry I'm late. I had an, ah, emergency," I say, adjusting my bra strap. I am a professional, dammit.

"Whatever. You're on time," the woman grunts, and turns her back on me.

Everyone's a real sweetheart this morning.

I climb up the stairs to the stage, heart jackhammering in my chest, and sit down in the seat marked for me. My newest book, *Forbidden Desire*, is sitting right in front of me on a stand. Already, the women by the door have taken their seats, and the room is filling with cheerful smiles and excited faces.

I take a deep breath. *Be poised and calm, Julia. You can do this.*

"Hey there." I turn to find Shanna sitting next to me, wiggling her eyebrows."Hey." I smile, and she smiles back, and I smile wider, and she smiles wider back, and I'm pretty sure we're going to have to stop this soon because I think my face is going to rip. "Are you okay? Why do you look like you want to slather me in butter and eat me?" Granted, I'd eat anything slathered in butter. Even myself.

"Just proud of you." She throws an arm around me and kisses my cheek. "Congrats, you know?" She giggles.

Shanna never giggles. Wait.

"You remember where we were last night?" I say, grabbing her hand. Finally, her overjoyed smile eases somewhat.

"You mean you don't remember?" Her eyes widen.

"I would love to. Holy shit, remembering would be the sweetest thing right about now," I say. "What did I do?"

"I don't know," she says, now looking kind of freaked out. "After the club, I thought—"

"What club?" I ask, but we have to shut up. The moderator sits down at her podium: Brenda Summersby, queen of the Revolutionary spy romance.

We do a quick intro, running down the table. It's me, Shanna, Jane Morningside (real name Cathy Grimsby), and a couple of e-book only authors. The whole time we're all laughing and exchanging stories of researching espionage, my skull seems to be pounding.

Just make it to the end of the panel. Then Shanna can tell me all about the glorious things I did or, hopefully, didn't do last night.

"I think we'll take some questions," Brenda says, opening the floor for discussion.

A thirty-something woman stands up and asks Shanna about her *Babylon Corrino* series. While Shanna is talking about Hypatia Mercurado, alien queen, and her tortured backstory, I notice a guy in a suit enter and stand off to the side of the room. He looks fortyish, with thinning hair and a wilting moustache. Definitely not the typical romance reader, but hey, it's always nice to know you can move people outside the target demographic.

But the unnerving thing is . . . that he's looking at me. Constantly. Even when other people are speaking.

Nah. No. Nope. No way. This day has been hell enough already and it's only just started. I don't need *Men in Black* rejects following me around, making me even more paranoid than I already am. Maybe this guy just really likes my latest hero Jack Fathom and his naughty BDSM helicopter rides over Puget Sound. Anything is possible, man.

But then I watch as a guy in a full on security guard outfit enters and stands right beside Gray Suit, and I know I'm screwed. They're both staring at me now.

"Julia? Hello?" Brenda says. Oh, shit. I completely wasn't paying attention. The nice-looking lady in the audience is now staring at me expectantly.

"Sorry. I, er, had a blackout moment. Get those some-times. Vegas, you know?" I say. A ripple of laughter goes through the audience, but Gray Suit doesn't smile. Oh shit. "Unless I'm operating heavy machinery! Then my blood alcohol content is perfectly legal," I snap, looking at Gray Suit in a panic.

No one laughs at that one. In fact, it's kind of awkward. Like my life.

When the panel is over, I grab Shanna's hand. "Can you sneak out with me?" I mutter, keeping my head down and not making eye contact with the fuzz. Shanna, who is no one's fool, narrows her eyes at me.

"Is this about those guys? Julia, what is going on?" she whispers.

"Why don't you tell me?" I whisper-shout right back at her. "What did I do last night? Did I kill anyone?"

"No! I mean, I don't think so," Shanna says, eyes going even wider.

"Oh, fucking fantastic."

A man clears his voice right above us. Wincing, I look up and, sure enough, there's Gray Suit standing over me. He's got a wicked comb over, and a mouth set to permanent scowl.

I sit up, grinning brightly. Grinning. Always grinning. Even when it hurts.

Ow, my hangover.

"Can I help you?" I ask him, trying not to burst into tears and throw myself on his mercy. I succeed. Just.

"Ms. Stevens, I'm with hotel management. Would you come with me, please?"

Dear God, just tell me I didn't harm any kittens last night. Or operate a crane lift. Or sell anybody's organs on the black market. I am pretty sure I'll be fine so long as none of those things happened. Unless I crane-lifted a bunch of kittens after selling their organs on the black market, because there's no coming back from that shit. Then you join Hannibal Lecter behind a plexiglass wall for all eternity.

What were we talking about? Oh, right. Hotel management.

"Of course I'll come with you," I say, getting up slowly. See, nothing wrong here, sir. Shanna looks at me with wide, freaked out eyes, but I wave her concern away.

It's not like they're going to put me in jail, for God's sake.

THEY PUT ME IN JAIL. Holy shit. They put me in fucking jail. Call my mother and tell her I love her, call my father and tell him I can't loan him any more money, call my grandmother and tell her she needs to stop day drinking. I am never getting out of this.

All right, on the plus side, it's not like I'm sitting in a city jail. It's a hotel holding room, which basically means beige-colored carpet with beige walls and a beige futon. In Vegas, if they put you in beige, you are seriously fucked. No sequins or rhinestones anywhere means I must have done something abominable.

Okay. I take three deep breaths, trying to achieve my zone neutrality. Or something. I don't know! *Okay, keep calm, Julia. Maybe they can help. Maybe they can help piece together whatever insane stuff you did last night. Or rather, the weird shit that your David Tennant personality did.*

On second thought, maybe talking about *Doctor Who* would be a very bad thing right now.

The door opens, and Gray Suit—his name's actually

Todd, but I'm sticking with Gray Suit—enters and sits down in a chair opposite me.

"Now Ms. Stevens—"

"I'm not going to prison," I blurt out. "I'm too soft. I watched *Orange is the New Black*. I don't want to eat tampon sandwiches."

Gray Suit blinks slowly. "Okay. I'll bear that in mind."

"Look, what the hell am I even doing here?" I snap. *Great, Julia. Get snippy with the authorities. This'll go down swimmingly.* "What is happening?"

Gray Suit sighs. "It's about what you did last night, Ms. Stevens."

6

NATE

I THOUGHT a cup of coffee would kill this bastard behind the eyes, but apparently I was wrong.

I'm sitting in the Café Bellagio, a high-ceilinged room with a faux French country furniture design and a loud carpet pattern of crimson red and abstract gold lines. I'm sitting here, rubbing my temples and wanting to die, while Tyler talks about . . . something. Probably something related to sex, but I'm barely paying attention right now.

Vegas is the capital of noise. The faux European ambiance does nothing to inspire a restful atmosphere. There's a sea of people all around us, people taking pictures of everything with their phones and yelling to each other. Every shouted word is like a bomb going off in my brain. I swear, I think my head's about to explode.

"Dude, that Shanna girl was fucking rad," Tyler says, sucking down some kind of papaya cold press concoction. I don't even know. "Writes about aliens, huh? Kinky ray gun submission fantasies. Princess Leia in a gold bikini. Oh yeah." He waggles his eyebrows.

I have no idea what any of that means. At least Mike and Stacy are here to even things out.

"I don't know, Tyler. You seemed pretty into that older lady, the one with the really filthy mouth?" Stacy says, laughing. She and Mike are sitting side by side, his arm slung around her chair. Something about that image of closeness right now just makes my head hurt even more.

"I mean, sure. But, uh, she's old enough to be my mom," Tyler says. Is it just my imagination or does he sound defensive?

"Nate. You look like you've come back to the land of the living," Mike says. He whistles. "You must've gotten shitfaced last night. Hope you had a good time." He's giving me knowing eyes.

"You know what I did last night?" I ask, feeling desperate. "Where I was?"

My total sincerity makes them stop laughing. Stacy puts a hand over her mouth.

"Oh, honey. Blackout drinking? That's fucking danger-ous," she says. Mike leans in over his half-eaten eggs Benedict.

"Dude. How bad is your hangover?" he asks.

I'm about to tell him everything—me waking up with Julia, the gaping holes in my memory—when there's a cough right next to my chair. Someone is standing beside me, waiting for my attention.

"Sir, excuse me," the man says. I look up. My double vision condenses down to one image of a gray-suited man with steely eyes. "I'm Todd Andrews, hotel management. I need you to come with me, please."

"What's wrong?" I ask. It's taking a moment, but my lawyer senses are kicking back into gear. Mike, Stacy, and Tyler all share freaked out looks.

"It's about a video, sir. Security has a few questions."

OF COURSE JULIA'S HERE, too. I sit down next to her in a small room at a stainless steel table. Mr. Andrews sits opposite us. A video monitor is off to the side, and my stomach lurches. Whatever I'm about to see, I doubt it'll be good.

"What's this about?" I say again. Julia nods and points at me.

"Him. He's a lawyer. He knows lawyer tricks." She squints. "You *are* a lawyer, right? Yesterday's kind of a blur."

Thanks for the help. "Yes. I'm a lawyer," I say, my voice flat. She rolls her eyes.

"Thank you, wielder of the mighty sword of condescension."

"If I can have your attention," Andrews says, and hits play.

I watch, and there I am. With Julia. At—checking the timestamp—five-thirty in the morning. Well, that's something at least. Now I know where I was just before dawn. We're in the enormous Bellagio fountain, dancing right on the lip of it. Dancing. I kind of want to bang my head on the desk, but lawyerly cool must be maintained at all times. Especially when Julia is making more panicked and "I'm guilty" faces with every passing second.

Now we're stripping down to . . . okay, nothing. I join her in the fountain, lurching around. Now she's got her arms around my neck, and we're kissing. Deeply. Passion-ately. And my hands are very actively going down her body.

We each snatch glances of the other out of the corner of our eyes. I can't remember anything about this, and it's clear she can't either.

Finally, mercifully, the video ends. Andrews turns to us, his lips pursed in victory. "Would you care to explain, Mr. Wexler? Ms. Stevens?"

"Okay, so—" Julia begins, and I know she's going to incriminate us hopelessly.

"Is that the only footage you have?" I ask, putting my clasped hands on the table. Business. Professional. Pitcher of iced drinking water. Pretend we're back in my office on Wacker Drive. Pretend you have tickets to the Bears after legally destroying the man sitting right in front of you.

"Yes," Andrews says, narrowing his eyes. "What's your point?"

"There is no way to be certain that those images are of myself and Ms. Stevens. The picture is too grainy. It would be impossible to accurately identify facial features."

Beside me, Julia's eyes are bulging and she's biting her lip. But she starts nodding.

"I can't tell, honestly. No way to be sure," she says. Good.

"I'm pretty damn sure," Andrews says, but he's looking a little uncertain. "We have footage of you two entering the hotel lobby twenty minutes later. Wet."

I'm sure he does, but I shrug. "We were at the Mandalay Bay, attending a pool party. I believe we came home sometime close to six."

"I remember. Definitely around that time," Julia says. "Pool parties. Vegas, right?"

"Right," Andrews says, though his face is falling. I'm sure he doesn't believe it, but again, there's no way to prove that there was no pool party. And if I call my contact over at Mandalay Bay, he'll tell them I was there the entire day. No lie is too big for the lawyer who saved him from fifty million in alimony.

"Unfortunate coincidence, isn't it?" I ask. Now to go in for the kill. "Considering you apprehended myself and Ms. Stevens in front of colleagues and friends, your hotel has done significant harm to our reputations."

"I may not be able to work again," Julia says, her voice mournful. She even sniffs and wipes her eyes. Good. A little high school playish, but effective.

Andrews freezes; he knows he could get sued.

"Imagine my children, out on the street, freezing in the winter snow," Julia moans, laying her head on the table.

Okay. Don't overplay it.

"You have children?" Andrews asks. I press my foot on top of hers under the table, telling her to play it cool. She responds with a swift kick in the shin, and I have to bite my tongue to keep from shouting.

"Kittens. Three kittens," Julia sighs. Cat lady. I was right. I usually am.

"The point is, you should let us go. Chalk it up to a misunderstanding. I don't want to take any kind of action," I tell Andrews, my voice as cool and smooth as silk. "I would like to spare you from that kind of embarrassment."

Andrews squares his jaw, and I have a moment where I fear I've overplayed my hand. Even I have to acknowledge that arrogance is one of my failings. But instead of pushing it further, he nods once and grunts.

"All right. I'd recommend staying clear of the fountains for a while. Just to be safe." He looks from Julia to me. We're both the image of silent cooperation.

With that, Andrews rises up and buttons his coat. Julia sighs, batting her eyelashes. Her eyes are dewy.

I have to admit it—once she stops the larger than life theatrics, she's a damn good actress.

"Thank you so much," she sniffles, and we walk out of the room. She even slips her arm through mine, playing up to the idea of being desperately in love. Cute. Once we're back in the hotel hallway, we pull apart so fast she nearly rips my sleeve.

"Careful. This is Armani," I snap. Julia yanks me to the side, puts her hands on her hips, and frowns.

"Okay. What the hell happened last night?" she asks. Her face flushes pinker.

Despite all my annoyance, I have to force myself not to notice how sexy she looks when . . . wait. Flushed face. I have a memory of that, a quick one. My expression must change, because Julia notices.

"What? Keep me updated on the brilliant thoughts coming in over the wire."

"I don't know what happened. But now I'm worried," I say, checking over my shoulder. We don't need Andrews to see us conspiring together in the hall.

"Why? Think I gave you the clap?" she deadpans.

"No, of course not! Wait. You don't have it, do you?"

Oh shit. Tell me we used a condom, if we did anything. That's all I ask.

"I kind of want to say I have a bunch of communicable

diseases just to see the look on your face." She groans and pinches the bridge of her nose. "Look. Let's get a coffee and talk it over. All right?"

"Fine," I say. "We can't take too much time." I check my phone. Half past ten. "My friends' wedding starts in less than seven hours."

"You don't have to spend your day running around with me, you know," she says, folding her arms.

"Actually," I say, "I do." Because if that video was any indication, Julia Stevens and I had a hell of a good time last night. And on the off chance any of that good time was illegal, it's probably in my best interest to find out what happened.

"YOU THINK WE COMMITTED CRIMES?" Julia asks, her eyebrows shooting up. She blows on her mocha, a smile spreading over her face. She even bounces a little in her seat. "Oh my God. This is epic. Sort of *Bonnie and Clyde*, but we don't get shot at the end. Wait." She rummages through her pocket—of course her dress has a pocket—and pulls out her phone. The phone case is the same blue box weirdness she got tattooed on her ass. Naturally. "Vegas Bonnie and Clyde would be delicious for my new romantic thriller series."

"Would you concentrate?" I take a sip of my mint tea. I don't imbibe any caffeine after my first cup of coffee. I don't like to be dependent on anything. "Skinny dipping might be the least of our worries. If we were out of control, and people find out, it could do damage to our careers."

"Maybe to yours, O Great Divorce Attorney. My fans

would probably eat it up. They like to think I've culled all the wild, romantic escapades in my books from experience."

But Julia's not as flippant as her remarks would make her sound. She's chewing on her lip, a clear tell of nerves. I stare at her mouth. Her full, soft lower lip does look very bitable.

Don't let your dick lead you around, Wexler. So far this girl hasn't brought you anything but migraines and a possible criminal record.

"Let's start with you. What's the last thing you remember doing yesterday?" I ask. I grab a paper napkin, take my pen out of my coat pocket, and get to work. When discussing techniques and strategies with clients, I like to sketch out the plans. It helps when I see something in front of me.

Julia groans.

"I don't remember doing you. That's a shame." She puts her chin in her hand. "You were probably good, given the video footage."

How the hell do I respond to that? "We couldn't see the expressions on our faces," I say at last. Clearing my throat, I continue. "No way to get a proper reaction."

"No, but from your body language, I could tell you were *very* excitable." She grins and chews on an almond biscotti.

If I didn't have to make damn sure I haven't murdered anyone . . . . *It's okay, Nate. You just have to keep it together until we piece together last night's timeline. Then you're out.*

"Again. What do you remember?" I say. Apparently I'm being too businesslike about this, because she sighs in annoyance.

"Wow. Lighten up, Nate. I'm just as worried about this as you are." She frowns.

"Clearly you're not, because I'm the one trying to make a plan and you're the one making jokes." My headache is coming back, a dull pounding behind my eyes.

"I like to think of it as 'I'm trying to keep us calm.' You're dead certain we're headed to Alcatraz."

"Alcatraz isn't a functioning prison anymore," I say.

"You're a functioning prison," she says.

"That doesn't make sense!"

"Neither does splashing and frolicking and groping your dick in the Bellagio fountain, but in case you hadn't noticed, there's a whole buffet of *doesn't make sense* going on right now. So load up your plate, grab the crab legs before they run out, and eat." She huffs, running a hand through her eternally frizzy hair. "All right. I remember meeting everyone for the Cirque de Soleil show here—O, I think, that's the name. Then we went for a drink afterwards before going to dinner. That's all I—"

"You remember the bar?" I ask.

She screws up her face. "Yeah, the Lily Bar and Lounge. How many bars does one hotel need, you know?" She shrugs.

"Let's go," I say, turning and heading like a shot for the lobby. I slow down, pause. Julia sidles up next to me.

"You don't know where it is, do you?" she asks, smiling sweetly.

I hate Vegas.

"I REMEMBER YOU," the bartender says, grinning at Julia.

He's a handsome guy, mid-thirties with thinning blond hair.

He wipes down the bar while I stand beside her. The place is intimate, wood-paneled walls with some purple velvet hangings. It's closed, but he's setting up for the afternoon.

"This your boyfriend? Fast work." He winks at Julia, who laughs a little.

Somehow, their flirtation irritates me.

"Can I ask you a crazy question?" Julia says, putting her chin in her hand and looking up at the guy. That would be disarmingly attractive if I didn't know her. "What did I do after I came here last night?"

"You kidding?" the guy says, raising an eyebrow. He leans against the bar. "You didn't have that much to drink here."

"I'm guessing I did shots somewhere along the way. This bar was the only thing that stood out in the haze," she says. God, she even winks. "Or maybe this bartender."

"Bam." He claps a hand over his chest and laughs. "Right through the heart."

We're wasting time here. That's why their flirting is getting on my nerves. Probably.

"Can you help us or not?" I say. I'm trying for glassy, lawyer cool. The bartender smirks.

"All right. You said you were going to some Brazilian steakhouse. Vio, or Via, or something like that. It's down along the Strip. Not too far."

"Thanks," I say, turning around at once and heading off. I have to wait as Julia talks with the guy a little more, then finally decides to get up and join me. She sashays a little, a pleased smile on her face. "Anything else coming back to you?" I ask.

"Oh, it's coming back all right." She points to herself. "The flirt machine hasn't gotten rusty." Then she does some kind of victory dance.

Why the hell couldn't Stacy and Mike have gotten married in Evanston?

7

JULIA

"WEREN'T THOSE CLOWNS HILARIOUS?" I say as I slice away at a thick, juicy steak. It's a healthy pink and deep red in the center, absolutely perfect. "I want to know how they stayed afloat on the roof of that house!"

O at the Bellagio is complete magic, all water acrobatics and high dives. Probably my favorite Cirque I've ever seen.

The girls all nod, sipping drinks and making orgasm noises over the quality of the steak. Sometimes it doesn't suck to be me.

"Glad you got to see some funny clowns," Shanna says, winking as she clinks glasses with me. "That guy this afternoon was more of a sad clown."

I laugh, then rub my forehead and sigh. That Nate Wexler asshole really got under my skin. It took a glass of champagne at the hotel bar—and the attentions of a really cute bartender—to get me out of my funk. Now I'm riding high on a cloud of good booze, good friends, and the Vegas lights. Nothing can beat this.

Wait, no. Dancing. Some kind of salsa dancing on the floor with a live band will add spice to any evening. The band strikes up, and the lights dim a little. Shanna and I laugh, and she grabs my hand.

"May I have this dance?" she says, batting her eyelashes. I pretend to swoon.

"I thought you'd never ask," I say. We all get out of the booth and head to the floor.

The men onstage are dressed in some kind of cultural costume, with blinding white shirts and big sleeves. They wink and greet us as we start moving to the music; everyone likes to have their work appreciated. Seconds later, I'm spinning around next to Shanna. Meredith and a couple of other authors—Daphne and Toni—appear to be going under a limbo stick on the other side of the room. I don't think salsa or limbo are really Brazilian in origin, but eh. I'm not going to complain.

"Ten four," Shanna whispers in my ear. She bumps her hip against me. "Someone's dancing up to you." And then she leaves me, just like that, twirling back into the crowd.

"What?" I say, not understanding. Until I feel a presence brush up right beside me, and then it's all super clear.

"Hi there," someone whispers in my ear.

There's this insane moment where I turn around and expect it to be Nate Wexler. That would be the cherry on top of this day. In fact, there's a small part of me that hopes it's him. Just so I can get the opportunity to stomp on his foot, of course.

But it's not Nate, not at all. A tall man with shaggy blonde hair and a goatee is dancing right next to me. He's doing a white guy hip swivel that counts as salsa dancing to the Nordic set, but I'm not going to make him feel bad about it. He's close, very close, but not that thing where he dry humps your leg while you shake your ass. Classy. That's a promising start.

"I wanted to dance with the sexiest girl in the place," he says in my ear. He grins.

"Um. Hi," I say. I even give a small, dorky wave.

I'm not really sure what to say or how to dance or how to think words right now. I've never had a *Dirty Dancing* meet you on the floor kind of moment before. I spin around, looking for Shanna. When I find her, I give her wide *help me* eyes. She frowns, points at the guy, and mouths, "Talk to him!" She wears that little crooked expression of hers, the kind that makes me feel like she's a tiny bit sorry for me.

All right, then. I can do this. I've been out of the game a long time, sure. Okay, like over a year. Most nights I'm working on a deadline, getting a beer with friends, or catching up on Netflix. Maybe I've been a little overly cautious about going out there and having a good time, and this is my chance. I've got to get back in to the flirting pool, one toe at a time.

I just wish I knew what to say. Like, how do I interest a guy, seduce him, make him think I'm sexy and desirable?

I mean, if only I were a romance author or something, duh. *Come on, Julia! Screw flirting, your professional reputation is at stake here! I mean, kind of!* I turn back around, this time with a smile playing on my lips. I also shake my hips a little more, just a white lady trying her damn best. I try for coy and mischievous. Coy and mischievous are right up this guy's street. He moves a little closer, letting his hands drift down to my hips. I do a little shake. I think he likes it.

"I'm Julia," I say, putting a hand on his shoulder while we dance. I press myself close, feel the heat of his body through his white T-shirt. In my fantasies, he'd be dressed up a little more. Ooh, like in an Armani suit, elegant and aloof. And then he'd open his mouth and tell me his name was something exotic, something like—

"My name's Derek," he says. Okay, that puts a bump in my fantasy. But the next words out of his mouth are, "Buy you a drink?" I already like where this is going.

What did Lola Sinclair say when she first met Archer Valmont in *Sizzling in Seattle*?

Well, she had his dick in her mouth in the first ten pages, so maybe not much in the way of dialogue.

But nothing wrong with pretending to be Lola, is there? If nothing else, girl knows how to get the job done.

"Drink?" Derek asks again, a little concerned look on his face.

Crap. I'd done the *go to another dimension* writing blackout thing. I've been told my eyes cross when I do that. I toss my hair and return myself to the here and now. Lola it up, Julia. Let's do this.

"Love one," I purr into his ear. Derek likes that. He sweeps me off the floor, finding us a cozy little booth in the corner. I slide in, and he moves in after me, casually circling his arm behind, then slowly around me. I'm a goddess right now; everyone should come and offer gifts of chocolate and mojitos. That's my currency.

"Do you live around here?" Derek asks, once we get a couple of shots going. Mmm, shots are a sensational treat

I've denied myself since college. The tequila burns on the way down; that's good.

"I'm here on business." I grin, looking up at him slyly. "Maybe mix it with a little pleasure while I'm in town."

"Pleasure. I like the sound of that," Derek says, running his hand down to linger on the small of my back. I push my chest forward, showing off my very nice cleavage. I'm not modest; a girl has to know her assets. Derek appreciates it. "What kind of business are you in?" he asks.

"International espionage." Well, that was what Lola was doing—trying to crack Archer's heavily encrypted files and getting more than she bargained for in the process. "I have to create a distraction at the Venetian hotel while my team breaks in and pulls off an elaborate heist."

I take another shot of tequila and lick my lips in what I hope is a sexy way. Seems to be, because Derek's hand travels a little further south and traces across my ass.

Sexy. Be Lola. Experiment, dammit. "Oh, Mister . . . Derek. You are so bold," I drawl.

"And you're, like, super fucking hot," he says, leaning in for a kiss. His breath is stenchy with liquor. Before he can claim his kiss, I laugh and kind of push away from him. That brought reality crashing back in a kind of hard-hitting way. Derek doesn't seem deterred. Well, if he gets too out of line, I know a good karate chop. Self defense forever, kids.

"What do you say?" he asks, trailing his fingers around my ass, my hip, heading for . . . *hello there.* I cross my legs. He pulls out his wallet, and takes out a plastic key card. "I'm in Paris."

I almost tell him that he has his cities mixed up, when I realize he means the hotel. "Oh," I say, super eloquently.

"What do you say, gorgeous?" He leans in for a kiss again, his mouth open, his lips . . . kind of dewy looking, actually.

In the haze of booze, part of my body is screaming *yes*, cavorting around and waving pom poms. Because it's been a long time. Like a long, long time. Too damn long. But at the same time, much as I'd like to be Lola, Derek's not exactly Archer. My wonderful image of me as a spy mistress falling for a debonair billionaire's charms goes pop. I get an image of myself as I probably am right now, a sad, drunken thirty-something looking for validation from a guy who's so bombed he's about to pass out.

That's not what I want my first time back in the saddle to be.

"Thanks," I say, switching my voice from seductive Lola to chipper me. I even grab his hand and shake; it's pretty limp. I'll take that as a sign that any bedroom shenanigans would be pretty lacking. "I, uh, gotta go. That espionage won't, eh, espionage itself. Bye."

I slide out of the booth and walk back to the dance floor before Derek can answer. I also wobble a little, because man, that tequila was good and strong. Where the hell is Shanna? I turn around and around, but it's a whirling madhouse of limbo, maracas, and what appears to be a matador egging on an actor dressed in a bull costume.

I'm just going to say it; this ambiance is very inaccurate at representing the great and rich culture of Brazil.

I burp, very sexy.

"Julia!" Shanna calls, waving to me from the bar. She

and the other ladies are laughing it up with what appears to be a bachelorette party. I'd know those plastic tiaras and neon glowing necklace penises anywhere. I go over to them and hop onto a stool. I also slide off once and have to pull myself back up. Okay, maybe I'm a little drunk. But who cares? I'm awesome.

"Oh my God, you're Julia Stevens?" the woman sitting next to me says, clutching my arm. She's got to be the bride; her tiara has a nice little lace veil on top. She's an attractive woman, probably in her early thirties, with sleek dark hair and a healthy tan. "I'm sorry, it's just . . . you're kind of my favorite author. I had no idea the Romantic Style convention was happening this weekend. I couldn't have planned a better bachelorette party!" Her eyes are actually shiny with tears.

A slow, warm happiness spreads through my body. My favorite part of conventions is meeting with fans, hands down. And if those fans are about to walk down the aisle to a happy future of their own? Even better.

"All this is going to my head," I say, grinning. I clutch onto the bar as well, to stop the room from lurching back and forth. "Or maybe that's just the booze."

"I'm Stacy Kaufman." She shakes my hand, then gives me a hug. "Oh my God, nothing but romance authors. This is my favorite part of the night!"

"Then you are having one shitty bachelorette party," Meredith says, knocking back a shot of something and putting the empty glass down. She's accumulated quite a collection, but she still looks steady as anything. Taking a long drag on a cigarette, Meredith winks at us. "But if it's a bachelorette party that makes my author money, I think it's a great time."

"When are you due to walk down the aisle?" I ask.

"Tomorrow. I'm half afraid we'll all be too wasted to get married," Stacy laughs. "Luckily, our hotel's the venue."

"Which one?"

"The Bellagio. Very *Ocean's 11*," she says proudly.

A woman after my own heart.

"I hope you have a lot of sexy shenanigans before the night's over," I tell her, putting my elbow on the bar and my cheek in my hand. I'm getting a little sleepy tipsy. It's the kind of buzz where you either need to party harder and wake up a little, or you go home and go to sleep. I'm thinking it'll be the latter, but then Stacy's eyes light up.

"Listen, why don't you all come along?" Stacy says, bouncing excitedly in her seat. "We were thinking of maybe finding a Chippendale show somewhere."

"Oiled men with their shirts off, gyrating to music." I put a hand over my heart in mock horror. "Do you really think I'm that kind of girl?"

"Yep," Stacy says. We both burst out laughing. I like this woman.

"I'm absolutely down for anyone getting naked, of any gender," Shanna says, grabbing her purse. "I'm all about equal opportunity for hot people."

"You've convinced me. Let's go," I say.

Stacy whoops and nearly falls off her barstool. We all pay for our drinks and head for the door. The night air is sultry, still so warm that I'm starting to feel silly for having brought a sweater.

Stacy fishes around in her purse, and a look of worry crosses her face.

"You okay?" I ask her. Daphne, Meredith, and Toni are

already dancing down the street, talking about a Mexican hat dance. I swear, this restaurant really doesn't know all that much about Brazilian culture.

"Shit. I forgot my phone. I left it." She stops and smacks herself on the forehead. "Dammit! My fiancé has it."

"Here, type his number in my cell." I hand her my trusty iPhone with its blue police box TARDIS case, and Stacy dials. While she talks to her fiancé, Shanna and I look at each other.

"Are you ready for well-muscled, oiled men with their shirts off?" she asks.

"Dirty jobs for dirty minds." Our high five connects.

"Bye, babe," Stacy says, and hangs up. "Okay," she says, handing over the phone. "Let's just stay put. They're coming for us in their car. It'll be hard to miss— they're rolling down the street in—"

"Ahoy fair maidens! Let's get shitfaced!"

That voice sounds familiar. A stretch Hummer pulls up alongside the curb. A smiling, frosted hair tipped guy is standing out of the sunroof, waving enthusiastically. I remember him; Tyler, that nice bro type who was with Mike and . . . .

Oh, fuck me. And not in the nice way, where I have two orgasms and someone makes me breakfast in the morning. The door opens, and Mike and that douche lizard Nate Wexler get out. At least this time, Tightass isn't wearing his impeccable fucking suit. He's in jeans and a black T-shirt. Looks kind of hot, honestly.

I'm not staring. I don't stare at jerks, even if they're hot.

"Hey babe," Mike says, kissing Stacy as she throws her

arms around his neck. "Needed a rescue?" He hands her a phone, grinning.

"More like a pick-up from a studly man. I do my own rescuing, thank you so much," she teases, and gives him another kiss. Mike laughs.

I've spent enough time writing real love to know it when it's standing right in front of me. I smile, though I have to force it a little when the Tightass Known As Nate walks over to me.

"So. You're joining us?" he asks, hands in the pockets of his jeans.

Now that he's closer, I get an even better look at his body in casual wear. And it's probably the tequila talking, but he's in pretty good shape. That black tee clings in the right ways to his torso. I can pick out the definition of sculpted pecs, and his arms are built. I admit it; I let my eyes trail down to a very firm ass in his well fitting jeans. No boxers hanging out with this boy; class all the way.

"Stop inspecting me," he grumbles. I give an over-the-top wink.

"Like to see what you're working with, Wexler." I sashay into the limo, squeezing in beside Tyler and Stacy. Tyler waves in the other girls, and Meredith ends up sitting beside him.

"Hey, Merry. Lookin' good," he teases.

Damn, Meredith may be old enough to be his mother, but she's bold enough to make him forget that fact. She arches a perfectly plucked and penciled eyebrow. It's like Joan Crawford going after college frat boys.

"You being a naughty boy so far?" she asks, giving his knee an enthusiastic squeeze.

"You know it." Still grinning, Tyler pops a bottle of champagne.

The night's going along beautifully, so long as I can ignore Nate Wexler, certified lawyer and registered pain in the ass. He sits there with his hands on his knees, tense, like he's holding his breath and waiting for this night to be over.

"Where to next?" Shanna calls, now wearing a plastic tiara of her own.

"We were thinking a strip club," Nate says, with all the pain of a man who probably wanted the boys to have a sedate steak dinner and be in bed by eleven-thirty.

Aw. Poor baby.

"Yes!" Tyler shouts, clapping his hands. "Strip clubs love when you bring ladies in. They'll probably give us some free drinks."

"I'm not sure women enjoy going to strip clubs, Tyler," Nate says, the disdain in his voice so obvious even Stacy blows a raspberry.

"You're right. We like sitting at home, knitting, and watching Downton Abbey," she mocks.

And while I do love tea, crocheting, and the Dowager Countess, I agree with her. We're not a set of prudish wilting flowers.

"Bring on the ladies," I say, nudging Nate with my elbow. We eye each other. Again, I find myself falling into the magnetic blue of his eyes—just for a second, of course. I don't care how good-looking he is, though. I'm not into stiffs and snobs, and he is way both.

Nate squares his jaw, but he says nothing. Score one for me.

"The Palace Veil it is," Mike says, arm around Stacy's waist.

Everyone cheers but Nate and me. I know we'd both be happier if the other wasn't there. Ah well. When in Vegas, ignore the douches, let the good times roll, and always carry a spare set of panties in your purse, just in case. That's what Mom used to tell me.

Mom was fun.

8

NATE

YESTERDAY, 9:36 PM

THE PALACE VEIL is a little outside of the Strip, in a rundown looking part of the city. Neon lights flicker all around the outside, a squat one story with thumping music bleeding out into the night. Pictures of over-bleached and over-glossed young women, topless with black bars to cover the most essential bits, line the exterior.

The driver parks and lets us out. I have to stifle a groan as Tyler leaps towards the door, enthusiastic as a kid in a candy store made out of breasts.

"Most men like seeing naked women, you know," Julia says, giving me a smug smile as we walk toward the building. "Unless you're Data."

"What about my data?" I ask.

"Data, the humorless, literal android from *Star Trek: Next Generation*." She rolls her eyes. "You make my nerd heart sad, young Padawan."

"Is that also from *Star Trek*?" I ask.

She bursts out laughing. I'm going to stop asking questions.

We finally enter the club, the fog machine hazing the room to a degree where I can't even see the grimy floors or terrible cracked walls. Almost. It smells like Febreze and sweat in here—not the world's most hygienic combination.

At least Mike's having a good time. I think he's happier now that Stacy is here, actually. They're making out with enthusiasm over by the bar, and I turn my eyes away. Sometimes I think I'd like to find some flaw with Stacy, or more so, with their relationship. Something to point at, something that statistics tell me means it's never going to work out.

I'm a shitty fucking person, to quietly wish I could see some way for my best friends to be miserable.

I turn away from the others, trying to get a handle on my own thoughts. I want them to be happy. I know how much they need each other. But I can't help thinking that it doesn't matter how much love you start out with. Sooner or later, it all turns to shit. I know from experience.

Even after all this time, Phoebe will pop into my head unexpectedly. Sometimes the memories will be of the break up, her moving out of the condo, all the yelling that went on that incredibly shitty weekend when it finally ended. Sometimes I'll remember making love, or taking an afternoon walk through Millennium Park, my arm around her waist. Those are the moments that sting the worst, even more than the break up.

There's someone at my side. Someone with curly hair and, I have to admit, fantastic cleavage on display.

"Here," Julia says, shoving something into my hand. "Drink up."

"What is it?" I ask, making a face. I prefer a neat scotch when I can get one, and this is tall and ice cold.

"An iced tea, all the way from the wilds of Long Island," she answers. That's not really my drink. When I try putting it down, she grabs my wrist. "Think about it. You're holding a potent cocktail of oblivion. One might even call it a magic potion. Drink it, and the night goes by much faster. Pretty soon you wake up, and it's tomorrow."

She has a point.

"I'd say I get a lot hotter as well, but let's face it. I'm smoking already."

Yes, she definitely has a point. About the night going faster, not about . . . never mind.

I toast her, and swallow as much of the drink as I can in one gulp. It tastes like turpentine, but it's effective. I give it a minute . . . and instantly, the world hazes at the edges of my vision. I'm feeling all right. At least, better than I was before.

Hmm. This could be the beginning of a very fruitful partnership. Me and Long Island. Not really a man's drink, but I won't hand over my testosterone card just yet.

"Look at you!" Julia coos, patting me on the arm. I close my eyes; all this would be a little better without her condescension. "Shots?" she asks me. She wiggles her eyebrows.

Hmm. She already has a distinctly tequila smell about her.

"Sure you haven't had enough already?" I ask. She sticks out her tongue. Mature.

"Vegas is for making questionable decisions. That and accruing huge amounts of gambling debt. But I think we should stick with one vice at a time." We walk back to the bar. "What's your pleasure? I'm thinking some rum by way of Malibu."

I can handle only so many chick drinks in one evening. I take a Macallan instead, sipping it calmly. I'm in control, where I like to be. The booze starts a fire in my belly, and I can finally feel my shoulders relaxing, just a fraction. I don't want to get too drunk. I don't like to get too out of control. Ever.

The thumping sound from the speakers vibrates through me now, seeming to pulse in my bones. More dry ice smoke puffs over the stage, and some tall, well-endowed figures strut out, wearing high heels and not much else.

Tyler and Mike are standing at the edge of the stage. To my surprise, the girls are all crowded around as well, waving fistfuls of dollar bills. They seem more into this than the men are. The strippers come forward one at a time, dancing to some terrible house music. I watch one of them go into graceful splits. They're athletic, of course. One of them manages to turn herself upside down on the pole and take her top off at the same time, all the while in four inch heels. Impressive.

"Come on," Julia says. She appears almost instantaneously at my side, always when I least expect her. "You haven't given them any money yet. Don't be a holdout." She drags me over to the stage.

Sighing, I take a ten out of my pocket and toss it. The girl dancing up there crawls on her hands and knees, picks it up, puts it between her teeth, and then reaches for me, a smile playing on her face. I take a step out of the way. She pouts and moves on. Looking for someone to ask for a private dance session, no doubt.

I've had lap dances before, and I don't know how any man actually enjoys them. You get turned on by a woman you can't touch and leave feeling more frustrated than you were before.

Right now, I decide to go find Tyler. This is his version of Heaven. If he's not careful, he'll spend his life savings in this place.

"Are you sure you've got a pulse?" Julia asks, doggedly pursuing me.

"Is there a reason you're asking?" I growl.

She gives a dismissive wave. "She was hot."

"Are you an expert judge of other women's hotness?" I mutter.

"Romance expert, darling. Of course I am," she says, actually nudging me with her hip. Then she starts laughing, tilting her head back. Apparently too many shots will do that to you. "Besides, no red-blooded heterosexual man can contain himself when a woman is humping a pole in time to some Sia club music. It's common knowledge."

"Any woman?" I say, arching my brow. If there's one woman I doubt I'd ever have an erotic fascination with, it's an overly sparkly romantic. "Prove it. Why don't you dance?"

"What?" Even in the flashing lights of the club, I think I see her pale a little. Excellent.

"You heard me." I lean in and speak into her ear. "Or are you afraid to put your own theory to the test?"

"One thing I was always good at in science lab." She juts out her chin and pushes out her chest. Which, I have to admit, is pretty noticeable. "Experimenting. How else would I have ever sewn a fetal pig's head onto a frog's body?"

"You're kidding, right?" I think that disgusting Long Island iced tea is rippling in my stomach.

"Wouldn't you like to know?" She tosses her hair and runs over to the stage. I have to admit it; Julia has a way with people. She waves one of the strippers over and manages to convince her to lean down for a conversation.

I must be widely grinning, because Mike shows up at my elbow one second later.

"What did you do?" he asks. No joking here. He follows this by a quick punch in the shoulder. "Seriously, man. What's she doing?"

"You'll see," I tell him, feeling smug. Julia Stevens will fall on her face in front of everyone, then stop her incessant chirping and preening. It's the beginning of a good night.

Once the song ends, one of the strippers grabs a microphone.

"Let's give it up for a lady just passing through town, Juliet Sayonara," she says. All the bachelorette girls go wild. Julia takes to the stage, a little flushed. She's wearing a purple top, with a spangled black skirt and high heels that she's clearly a little unsteady in. She strikes a pose against the pole, and the music starts. It's some kind of slower, sultrier anthem, with a pulsing bass beat. This is going to be so embarrassing—

And then she starts to move, sliding down the pole

slowly. The movement is languid, sensual. She arches her back as she sinks lower, spreads her legs.

Christ. She gets up and spins, her hair whipping and spilling across her back. She looks over her shoulder and winks at the crowd. All the women eat it up, screaming for her, shouting "Sayonara!" at the top of their voices. Then Julia looks into my eyes.

Just like that, I'm helpless. Frozen. There's a smoldering heat in her gaze, something carnal, something primal. With one look, she could order me on my knees and I'd do it, whatever she wanted.

She spins about to face the front of the club. Then she swings around the pole, going lower and lower until she's practically lying on the floor. Where the hell did she learn to do this? Her skin glows softly beneath the lights, a delicate sheen of sweat visible from her exertion. She crawls over to one man standing by the stage. He stands there, gaping, with money in his hand. Licking her lips, she reaches out and pulls at his tie, loosening it. She grabs the dollar bills and stands slowly, pulling herself up inch by inch, her breasts pushed out, her skin flushed. Her lips are parted, her eyes lidded; it's the look of a woman on the brink of an orgasm.

And suddenly, I've got a hard-on. I grunt and grab onto the back of a chair. Julia slides one strap of her dress off her shoulder, revealing an expanse of beautiful, creamy skin. She grabs the pole and twirls around it again, moving her body in rhythm and time to the music. Slowly pulsing, like she's actually fucking the song.

I tighten my grip on the chair's back so hard I think I might actually snap the goddamn thing.

She's more limber than I thought. Way more fucking

limber. She stretches a leg up as high as she can, so that her heel is almost level with her head. It's not perfectly graceful—her leg shudders for a moment, stretching to its limit—but she finishes flawlessly. I catch a flash of her ass as she grabs her shoe, spins around the pole again, and lowers her leg.

The song ends. She's breathing heavy, and her eyes are dazzling. They're electric, pure fire, and as the applause explodes around her, she locks her gaze with mine and doesn't look away. She's challenging me. Daring me. And something possessive, something primitive, flames in my blood.

I need to fuck this woman. Now. And I think she wants me just as bad. Was I saying something before, about her being annoying? Overly sparkly? Fuck that asshole. Fuck him and send him right the fuck home. He had no idea.

I push through the crowd, hurry over to the stage and help her down.

"Great job!" people say around us, but all I know is Julia's hand finding mine. Her eyes tilt up the hazy, wanton expression is still there. She needs me. Her body is pressed up against me, her tits popping out of her low cut top. We walk away, finding a dark corner, a place no one can see. There, I snake an arm around her waist, press her against me. Julia gasps, feeling my hard-on through my jeans.

"I think someone lost the bet," she whispers, her lips just—just—grazing mine.

"Fuck the bet. Where can we go?" I grunt. In the confusion of the crowd, no one's gotten to us yet. My hands move along her bare arms, the touch of her skin electricity. I want to feel every inch of her naked body, want to hear her moan my name. I need her alone.

"Is there a closet around here?" she mutters. Her lips part, waiting for me to kiss her. And I will. Everywhere.

First, we find the fucking closet.

9
———

NATE

WE DUCK down the hallway and find a door. Flinging it open, we discover the room's empty. *Perfect.* I've never been so happy to see a janitor's closet in my life. I kick the bucket and mop out of the way as Julia enters, follow her, and slam the door shut. This closet is dark, and I put my hands on her. She gasps just with that contact. Julia pulls on a chain, and a light bulb comes to glaring life above us.

No. I reach up and yank it off.

"I want to fuck you like this," I tell her, sealing her mouth with mine. "In the dark." My lips brush hers. She tastes fucking glorious, the rich tang of alcohol warm on her breath, mixed with cherry lip gloss and the scent of arousal. She pulls me against her, hooks her arms around my neck, and climbs me.

Goddamn, this woman goes after what she wants.

I'm about to come just thinking about it.

"I don't have any condoms," I grunt as I help her pull her shirt over her head. Her bra is lacy; I toy with the edges of it, my fingers ghosting over the swell of her breast. She moans as I pull the bra down, her nipple going hard as I touch her. I flick my tongue across her peak, take her breast into my mouth and suck. Julia moans, keening deep in her throat. Even pinned up against the wall, she bucks against me, urgent. Her need is driving me on. Fuck.

"Hold on," she gasps, and gets me to let her down for a second. Fishing around on the floor, she comes back up. There's the sound of crinkling plastic.

Are those . . . glow-in-the-dark condoms?

"Bachelorette party. Waste not, want not," she breathes, then kisses me again, moaning when my tongue thrusts into her mouth.

She tugs at my shirt; fuck it. I pull it over my head, discarding it onto the dark floor. I'm blind in here, and there's only Julia's hands questing over my chest, trailing down my torso. She kisses my neck, flicks her tongue across my nipple.

Jesus. It's taking all my considerable will power not to fuck her right now.

I put my hand between her legs, feel how damp her panties are. While she gasps, I yank them down, so hard I'm sure it's a miracle I don't fucking tear them. I play with her a moment, circling my fingers around the swollen bud of her clit, earning a hard moan. But I don't touch her yet—not full on, at least. I drag those fingers up and down the seam of her pussy until they're soaked with her juices, once, twice, enough times to have her gasping in my ear and going mad against me.

Then I edge my fingers inside her, and try not to groan.

God, she's so wet. And tight. Her cunt hugs my fingers

like she's claiming them. But I have other things in mind, and start pumping. Slow at first, then harder, my thumb settling in the neighborhood of her clit and doing all I can to drive her anywhere as nuts as she's driven me.

Her arms go around my neck. "I'm going to come," she gasps. "Oh God." She grinds against my hand, her whimpers gaining volume, her pussy tightening around me.

Fuck.

"You can come when my cock is buried in you," I whisper into her ear. I pick her up and pin her to the wall. "Not before."

She gives me one of those ball-teasing groans in response, and I can't stand it.

My teeth tear free one of the condoms as my hand works at my zipper. Then—*shit yes*—she takes over. Her hot hand encircles my cock and I try, I really try, not to pant or moan or do anything that might reveal just how in control of this she is. Her tender hand around my dick is my fucking undoing. She strokes my cock down to the base and squeezes me damn near cross-eyed before dragging her hand up again. It goes like that for a few seconds. *Drag, squeeze. Drag, squeeze. Drag, squeeze.* It's heaven, but I know her pussy will be better, and I have to be inside her.

I take the condom out of my mouth, and I swear I mean to put the damn thing on, but my mouth finds the curve of her breast instead, and I pepper eager little kisses across her skin. My brain and body must have disconnected, because I know I need to be ready, but it seems more important this moment to slip a hand between us again. Feel her warm, wet flesh against my skin. So I do that, and she rewards me, her strokes coming harder, faster. Like she has a fucking line of sight to what I want, what I like, what makes me lose my mind.

"Fuck me. I can't stand it anymore," she whispers. Her lips whisper across my cheek, my neck, and her fingers circle the head of my cock, spreading the precum and furthering my path down insanity.

"I need you inside me," she says. She takes the condom, still in my hand, and rolls it over my shaft. Thank fuck one of us was thinking clearly. Or more clearly. I don't think either of us were doing much in the way of thinking.

I part her legs and ease her down, my cock drawing a line from her clit to the mouth of her pussy. She gasps and fists my hair, and I smirk at her as I sink into her warm cunt. Not all the way, just enough for her to get the idea. Then I pull out again and resume the wet path from her slit to her clit.

Fuck me, but she is tight. It's glorious.

"I want you to beg me for it," I whisper against her mouth, because, why not? I'm a masochist. But moreover, I really want to hear this woman beg. Tell me she needs my cock inside her, needs to come, needs me to be the one who makes her come.

She presses her lips to mine, hard and unforgiving. I grunt into her mouth as she rakes her nails down my back, my every nerve and molecule hypersensitive to her touch. Her kisses are almost as good as sex . . . but no, that has to be the alcohol talking.

I pull away at last, panting, then take a tour down her throat. Her taste, sweet and salty with sweat combined with everything *woman*, makes me harder.

I think it does, at least. At this point it's hard to tell.

Then her mouth is at my ear, and she's whispering furiously. "Fuck me right now. I'm begging you. Fuck me hard. Make me come. Please."

I can't respond, because she's dragged my face up to claim my likes again, her tongue plunging, stroking, and I know I can't hold on anymore, even if I wanted to. Which I don't, because I'm not *that* much of a masochist. After circling her clit with the head of my cock one last time, I drag myself between her pussy lips and finally—finally— ease my cock into her. And she's tight. So tight. Tighter than I thought, tighter than a woman has a right to be. Her cunt is pulling me deep. Her heat scorches me, and my rebellious brain—bastard that it is—whispers, demands, has the gall to tell me how much better it'd be if I were feeling her skin-to-skin. If that damn condom weren't necessary. If her naked flesh were wrapped around mine.

And then I think, well, it can't be better. It can't *get* better.

Can it?

Mother of fucking god, why did I tease myself so much?

I release a ragged breath, and when I can't go deeper, when I'm buried to the hilt, that breath becomes a moan. One she echoes.

Fuck. Her pussy is hot and perfect, squeezing me into oblivion. My name is a mantra on her lips, her hips following me as she tries to keep my cock inside her. But I need friction, and so does she. I pull back, savoring the feel of her wet, perfect flesh dragging along mine, then I sink back inside. I do this again, and again, memorizing everything about how she feels. And despite how intoxicating it is, fucking her in the dark, I find myself wanting to see her, watch her face flush and her lips part and her eyes go wide as she keeps chanting my name. As she comes all over my cock.

"Hold tight," I tell her, and start thrusting hard, until the air around us is a symphony of her rhythmic gasps, accented by the hot slaps of our bodies coming together. Julia bucks, claws at me, the little sounds she's making driving me out of my mind. I bury my face in her throat to keep from blurting something I'll regret later.

I can't see her, but I can feel her—her tits, her cunt as it welcomes my cock again and again. My balls are tightening and I know I'm close, but fuck, I need to feel her tumble first.

I keep her against the wall, one arm cradled around her waist as my other hand slips between our warring bodies. She inhales roughly when I encounter her slippery flesh, and goes crazy against me the second my fingertip brushes her clit. Her moves become faster, harder, more desperate. Her hair whips my face when she leans into me, and I swallow the cry I know was coming in a hard kiss.

"I'm going to come," she moans against my lips.

Good. I hope she screams when she does. My finger nudges her clit faster, not too hard but enough to get her there—to drive her over the edge—as I drive my cock inside her heat. I want her to feel me for weeks.

"Call my name. Come for me," I whisper, and bite down on her bare shoulder. It's not a hard bite, but it does its job. She jerks and gives me one of those whimpers again.

"Nate. Fuck me. Nate," she whispers, a song played

just for me. I feel the orgasm building inside of me, and as she spasms harder, her pussy tightens on my dick, I know she's just as close. I need her to get there first, or at least when I do. I press down on her clit, and it's the last whisper of my name that has the world exploding around me, a spinning void of light in the darkness.

"Fuck," I growl, unable to hold off anymore, my cock jerking as I spill inside her. Her pussy is convulsing around me, pulling harder and harder and she's saying my name like she's afraid she'll forget it. The sound of it —*Nate, Nate, Nate*—escalates until her voice has nearly drowned out the slaps our bodies make.

I pin her to the wall, panting hard, our hearts hammering against each other. Slowly, eventually, I return to myself long enough to lower her to the ground. She wobbles a little, still in those sexy, impractical heels. She leans her head against my chest, gasping.

"I didn't think I had it in me," she says.

"The dance? Fucking me?" I tilt her chin up and kiss her, hard. She groans deep in her throat.

"Both."

"I'm glad you had it in you," I whisper into her ear.

"I'm glad you had it . . . in . . . me?" she says, sounding confused. Then she starts giggling. It's a throaty, sexy sound. And I can't help it. I laugh along.

10

JULIA

"SO WE . . . " Nate says, trailing off as we stand in the stark daylight outside the world's most depressing looking strip club. The Palace Veil. Probably looks a lot better at night, with a ton of neon and the sound of loud music inside.

My temples are throbbing again, but it's not because of the hangover. It's the memories that've come flooding back since we stepped out of the car. I don't have everything yet. The memories are coming in mostly flashes, but they're there. Me dancing onstage, doing acrobatics I hadn't attempted since I was in pep squad. That explains why my legs were so sore this morning. Thank God yoga keeps me limber.

Then, of course, there's the janitor's closet after that. And all the things that happened in that closet. I could make a joke about getting dirty around cleaning materials, but I just don't have it in me right now.

Heh. In me.

Oh my God, what am I talking about?

"We went in the closet, and . . . " Nate pauses again. He seems as embarrassed about the whole thing as I am, which is at least one nice thing.

"You partook of my virtue, m'lord," I say, not meeting his eyes. When I get nervous, I go straight to Renaissance Faire speak. It's just easier to handle reality when I imagine I'm in a corset with a turkey drumstick, I guess.

Heh. Drumstick.

I'm going to hell.

Nate makes some kind of noncommittal noise. I peek over at him. He's the same as he was this morning, I remind myself, even though we now remember fucking. Same chiseled profile, same gorgeous but douchey hair, same dark blue gaze full of judgment. Same bad personality. Same insults. Insulting people isn't hot. I don't care what Lizzie/Darcy shippers believe; it's just common sense. But now my body is tingling in the slightest ways, my panties dampening the tiniest bit. Because I remember how that was, and it *was* hot.

Nate looks over at me as well, and maybe I'm crazy, but I think he's remembering it, too. Like, envisioning it.

"So. We know we came here. Where did we go next?" he says to me, studiously avoiding my gaze. Fine. I cross my arms.

"Before we go any further, I need one thing. Can you go inside and see if my, uh, purse is in there? I still can't find it." Or my laptop, but let's tackle one problem at a time. "It's got my ID, so I'm freaking out a little." I'm also blushing to the roots of my hair, remembering the taste of his mouth, the way he thrust into me so deep I could have passed out from pleasure. *Purse, Julia. Remember the purse.*

"Also I, uh, have a lunch meeting I need to get to. Like right now. Lunching. Pronto."

"I'll try to find your purse. Then I will be right back," he says stiffly, like a robot man.

Great. Of course he feels awkward. He's embarrassed about what happened last night, probably. I mean, so am I, of course. But at least I'm not making him feel gross and weird about himself.

Well, fuck him. I mean, I've already done, but still. Again. Let's do that. No, no let's not do that, Julia. What is happening to you?

My David Tennant Tenth Doctor subconscious is still spinning around, flipping brain dials and acting like a freak. Don't let him continue like that.

"Are you all right?" Nate asks, looking concerned. "Your eyes started darting back and forth."

"It's what happens when my id goes crazy," I say with a shrug. "I like to imagine my id's the Tenth Doctor. You know?"

"Excuse me?" Now he looks really scared. Great job.

"*Doctor Who*? David Tennant? BBC television show?" Okay, this really isn't helping my *I'm not crazy* thing. "It's on Netflix. Check it out sometime. Okay. Lunch away." I give a little swing of my arms as I say it and hop right back into the car to tell him to take me to the Bellagio ASAP, TYSM, WTF.

Thank God for my Uber account, or I'd have no money for the service.

"How am I getting back?" Nate says, standing there in the hot sun, the dust swirling around his feet, his shirt picking out the definition of his chest and abs, which I now remember running my hands along and boy howdy was that good . . . .

If David Tennant is my wild side, then the Ninth Doctor, played by Christopher Eccleston, is the calm and rational part of me. And right now, he has shown up out of the depths of time and space to tell me to stop drooling and get to my appointment.

"I'll send it back. Or call someone to come get you. Bye!" I wave and roll the window up as we drive away, listening to the competing British Time Lords duking it out in my head, fighting for supremacy. I actually imagine them, running around the consoles of my mind, pulling levers and arguing with each other.

"*You should have told him to find you later at the hotel,*" David Tennant says, jumping up and down and dodging around, looking adorable in his high tops and brown striped suit. "*Then you could force him into your car and drive around having hot sex! That's what I do with all my companions. Well, except for Martha. And Donna.*"

"*No!*" sensible Christopher Eccleston says, stepping in. "*You have to keep your distance. Suppose the Daleks invade, and you're emotionally compromised? And just think! Who knows if he's had his shots? What were you doing, having sex with a glowing condom?*"

Shut up, Doctor. You're not a doctor, for God's sake.

"You okay?" the cabbie asks, looking into the rearview mirror. A pair of fuzzy red dice hang from it, and a little Elvis bobblehead boogies on the dashboard. "Sounds like you're muttering to yourself in a bad British accent."

"Just a headache," I say, and stare out the window wondering how hard I'm losing my sanity.

"THERE SHE IS, my New York Times bestseller," Meredith crows, standing up and giving me a hug. "How are you, kid? Still hungover? Walking bowlegged?" She winks at me as I slide into the booth at the hotel restaurant.

God, I start blushing again, and just when I'd managed to stop. Just thinking about Nate's mouth on mine, his hands playing over my breasts while he had me pinned up against the wall . . . . Who knew cold fish lawyers were so passionate? This spurs another inner debate.

"Sorry," I say, shaking my head. "David Tennant and Chris Eccleston are arguing again."

"When aren't they?" Meredith says with a shrug. That's what I love about her. There is nothing too crazy for her to go along with. "Now Angela should be here in ten minutes or so—fucking editors, they're always running late at these things. We're pitching the *Starwood Resort* series. I'm thinking based on the success of *Forbidden Desire*, we'll have her salivating. She goes back to Ballantine, they throw some numbers around, and bam. I'm thinking we'll end up with a major deal."

"A major deal?" Damn, I'm almost floored at the thought of it. I'm pulling in good money with my royalties, but a high six-figure advance for the first time in my career? Shit. That'll buy a lot of crocheting needles.

"Speaking of high figures, how much did you have to part with in the divorce?" Meredith asks, raising an eyebrow.

Great. Good. I didn't need to be happy; my whole

luxuriating in the memory of good sex, it all goes up in smoke.

I fidget with my napkin, and Meredith clears her throat. "Sorry, kid. I just want to know how much of your hard-earned money Drew was able to snatch, that's all."

"You know, that doesn't make the situation sound any lighter," I deadpan.

"Maybe not, but I'd like to kick the schmuck in the balls." She takes a long pull of chardonnay while I suck down some ice water. Dehydrated. So dehydrated.

"Not too bad. Two hundred thousand in the end. Lump sum, though, so no monthly alimony payments."

Of all the shitty memories of my divorce, the shittiest probably has to be sitting across from Drew in a high-rise building in Milwaukee, staring at him in a too-snug suit with a too-snug collar, as he pouts while his lawyer explains how I have to keep him in the manner to which he's become accustomed. We had no kids, no huge medical bills. He was young, healthy, able-bodied, had a job. But he couldn't resist walking away with a little something extra. Not to get too morbid, but that image makes all of our fun, happy times—the night he proposed, our honeymoon at the Dells, moving into our first apartment—get tainted by association.

"Word of advice. Pre-nup next time," Meredith says, flipping open her menu and taking a look. "Okay. You warned me once about getting oysters in the desert, but I gotta tell you. I'm thinking I want some seafood."

I haven't quite moved on from that one special word.

"Pre-nup?" I say, laughing. "Won't need it. I think I'll become a wily, Casanova-like heroine. Hitting the Riviera, banging lots of hot men with indeterminate accents. A woman of mystery," I scan the menu and try not to remember my orgasm last night. I had to have been drunk. Okay, I mean, I know I was drunk, but I had to have been really out of my mind. No sex can be that good, especially not with a stranger in a janitor's closet that smells like ammonia. Especially not when that stranger happens to be a lawyer who also happens to be, shock of all shocks, a cold-blooded asshole. Even David Tennant agrees with me on this.

I wonder if that cold-blooded asshole ever found my purse. I wonder if I should hunt him down and find out. Give us another chance to talk.

I wonder why I like that idea so much.

11

NATE

THE HOTEL POOL sparkles in the hot noon sunlight. Scantily clad women frolic, splashing each other, laughing. The desert air is warm but not roasting, especially underneath the shade of this umbrella. You'd think this'd be paradise, my own personal Xanadu of beautiful bodies and poolside cocktails. Unfortunately, the whole brush with the law problem earlier this morning has kind of taken the fun out of this for me.

Besides, there's Julia. I'm remembering even more now. And that's more than a little distracting.

The sun is damn bright, but at least I'm wearing my sunglasses, so my headache isn't reaching epic proportions. While I sit with Mike in the shade, drinking a beer to try to get over my hangover before the ceremony, I focus. By focus, I mean I watch Tyler make a spectacular ass of himself. That's been happening a lot on this trip.

"Cannonball!" he yells, leaping into the pool while a bevy of giggling women shriek and get out of the way, squealing playfully.

Squealing. My temples throb.

When Tyler surfaces, he swims over to the side of the pool and lounges there, cracking a lopsided grin. "Ladies. Who wants to get with a cannonball *maître d'*?"

I think he means *maestro*, but I'm not about to correct him. I don't know what's worse: that he's saying those idiotic words or that the women appear to be falling for it. Two of them chat by him, giggling. One even runs her hand along his arm.

Has civilization come to this? Women throwing themselves at Tyler Berkley? Where did we go wrong?

"The hell, man. You need to lighten up. Why don't you get in the pool?" Mike asks, looking over at me with a beer in hand. The sight of alcohol makes my stomach ripple a little, even as the (now lukewarm) taste of it is helping my migraine somewhat.

"Not feeling it," I say, and pop a couple of Advil, which I'm sure is totally safe to take with beer.

I need it, though, partly because of this throbbing headache. Partly because since revisiting that strip club and remembering everything that went on in there, I keep thinking of Julia. Not the way she rolls her eyes, or how annoying I thought she was yesterday afternoon, but the feel of her skin, the taste of her lips, the way she sounded as I thrust inside of her. The way she dug her nails into my back, keening low in her throat as I fucked her, filled her.

See, right there. This is why I'm not swimming today. I don't need to fantasize about last night's hook up, pitch a tent in my swimming trunks, and then get in the water. This is a family pool.

Damn. I'm getting, ah, excited just thinking about it.

As I pretend to deliberately hunch over, giving myself time to go limp again, Stacy walks over to us. Apparently last night's party didn't faze her at all. She's in her hot pink bikini, towel around her waist, cowboy hat on her head.

"You boys awake at last?" she says, looking past Mike to me. Her forehead creases slightly. "You okay with the fuzz now?"

"Hilarious," I say, taking a sip of really warm, shitty beer. "Like I said, it was just a few questions."

I haven't told them about the fountain. I will never, ever be able to talk to them again if they find out. Mike and Stacy are the type to never let a funny story die, even if it was twenty goddamn years ago. At their children's future bar mitzvahs, I'll still get regaled by stories of my illegal skinny dipping.

Stacy purses her lips. She's not buying, but at least she's not going to push it.

"Babe, we need to go for lunch soon. I'm starving," she groans dramatically, hands on her stomach. Mike laughs and pushes up his sunglasses.

"You can really be this cool when you're hours from the altar?" he asks, mock serious.

"It's not an altar, it's a chuppah in Las Vegas. No worries at all." She brushes a hand through his hair. It's a familiar, intimate, happy gesture that I have to look away from.

"Get Casanova in here, then," Mike says, laughing as he watches Tyler pick up one of the shrieking girls and dunk her in the pool.

Stacy puts her fingers in her mouth and whistles, long

and shrill. Everyone at the pool startles, and Tyler actually tips over, going underwater.

"Ouch. That's at a level only dogs and future husbands can hear," Mike says, taking her hand and kissing it. He fakes her out and pulls her down into his arms. She laughs wildly.

God, they're so happy. They should remember they're in public. Love should be secret and shameful, something you apologize for experiencing.

All right, even for me that's a little harsh. But not by much.

"Dogs and future husbands are a similar breed," Stacy says, kissing Mike. He grins.

"Tongues hanging out all the time? Fleas?" He kisses her chin. "Shitting in the house?"

"Scruffy and adorable. And yes, pooping indoors, but nothing a little training can't fix." She wraps her arms around his neck. "It's why I love them. Dogs, I mean."

"Good. I was afraid you'd say you loved *me*. I don't know what I'd do with so much emotion."

While they keep kissing and giggling and I keep ignoring them, I look over at Tyler in the pool. Stacy's whistle did the trick; he's sloshing over toward us, leaving the girls behind.

I should be like him, fucking my way around the greater Las Vegas area. Maybe get a penicillin shot before-hand, of course. Clearly I'm capable of having hot, random sex with strangers. But that one particular stranger . . . .

I can't get Julia out of my head. Smart mouth and all, I wonder what she's doing right now. I want to feel her underneath me. Last time it was pitch black in that closet;

I want to see her eyes widen, her mouth open as she comes calling my name.

Or maybe I want to go upstairs and jerk off, because this hard-on situation is getting distracting.

"Hey. You." Stacy nudges me with her foot. She's seated on Mike's lap, her arm around his neck. "Things seemed to go well with Julia Stevens last night, huh?" She grins.

In addition to not talking about the fountain, I also don't want to go into the details of my blackout. That kind of thing makes you look sad in people's eyes. So I simply nod.

"She's . . . fun," I say at last. Stacy snorts.

"Only you can say *fun* like it's a disease." She looks at me, thoughtfully arching an eyebrow. Whatever's coming can't be good. "Hey, Nate. Guess what?"

"I can't even begin to guess," I say, as blandly as possible. "Your mind is a mystery. You're the Las Vegas sphinx."

"If we were at the Luxor, maybe. Listen, buddy," she says, leaning toward me. I have a bad feeling about this. "It's my wedding day," she says.

I get the feeling she's winding up to ask for something.

"And?" I say.

"And I want you to call Julia and invite her to have lunch with us." Stacy has that look in her eyes, the *I am prepared to fight and win* expression. She's a Chicago social worker, which means she has a ton of experience with impossible cases.

Lunch. With Julia. I groan, showing Stacy how much I'm opposed to the idea by my body language. I don't let her see the hard-on, though; I keep that as under wraps as much as possible.

"Whatever happened last night," I say, "whatever the hell it was in the moment, I don't think this is a woman I want to get entangled with."

Unless it's upstairs right now, in my suite, entangled in the sheets as we fuck each other senseless. That kind of entangling would be just fine.

Jesus, what the hell is happening to me?

"I don't think that's true," Stacy says, pursing her lips in a knowing smile. "Besides, it doesn't matter what you want. It's my special day. Bridal trump card, baby. Today, I get what I want."

"It's my weekend too," Mike says, pulling his bikini-clad fiancée against his chest and nuzzling her neck. She giggles. Mike's the only man alive who could make Stacy giggle. "Do I get a say in this?"

His tone's light, but I know Mike'll back me if I need it.

Ah, what the hell. Let me give Stacy something she wants for her big weekend, even if she has misguided, romantic notions about me and this girl.

"All right," I say at last. "Because I care so damn much."

"You're a treasure," Stacy drawls.

"I'll call her," I grumble, pulling out my cell. I think she's got her phone at least.

Stacy cheers and takes a long chug of Mike's beer. While he deals with his alcohol-swiping future wife, I wait as the phone rings once, twice. A strange feeling pulses through me; it's both lightness and unease. She may not pick up. She said she was having a lunch meeting anyway. Maybe I won't get to see her again. I can't tell if that's a relief or—

"Hello?" Julia's voice is wary. "Who is this?"

My heart beats faster. Goddamn it, why am I acting like some high school loser calling up his crush? *Pull it together, asshole.*

"It's Nate," I say. I clear my throat. There. Now I sound like a confident jackass. Exactly what I want. "Nate Wexler," I add in a voice that is five octaves deeper than it was a second ago.

"Oh, good. Your number isn't in my contacts. What's up? Did you find my purse?" she asks. Very business, very professional. She doesn't sound like she cares all that much.

What the fuck am I doing getting excited about this shit?

"Calling on behalf of Stacy. She wants to know if you'd like to have lunch with us," I say. My tone's casual. She can take it or leave it. Either way, doesn't matter to me.

"Oh. I mean, I'm eating now," she says, sounding surprised.

Right. Of course, she had a lunch meeting. I shrug.

"That's fine, I can tell Stacy—"

"But I'm a hobbit. We believe in second luncheon. Where should I meet you guys?"

Is it my imagination, or does she sound eager? That thought pleases me more than it should.

"A hobbit?" I ask.

"Please don't make me recite the entirety of *Lord of the Rings* to you. It'll take several hours."

"I know what hobbits are. Even I'm not that out of touch. We're over at the pool," I say, trying not to smile.

The hell is wrong with me? "Can't miss it. You'll recognize Tyler making an ass of himself."

Speaking of the buffoon, he pulls himself out of the pool and walks over to us, dripping.

"There's a sight that once seen cannot be unseen," she agrees.

Julia says goodbye and hangs up, and I take another swig of my beer as Tyler grabs a towel. My temples have stopped throbbing. Finally, my hangover appears to be lifting.

"Was that so hard?" Stacy says, giving me a damn smug smile.

"Not hard at all," I answer. And it wasn't hard. At all.

And that's the problem.

12

JULIA

"SO YOU SKIPPED out on the end of lunch with Meredith and your editor to go to another lunch with the guy you just now remember banging last night?" Shanna grins as we head into the restaurant. She throws an arm around me and squeezes tight. "I knew you were doing Vegas right."

Then she slaps my ass. Our friendship is deep and true.

"Yeah, yeah. Just enjoy the free food, all right? If we're all going out, I'm sure it's on Nate's, er, dime."

Oh God, I nearly said *on Nate's dick.* I nearly said it. I'm going to hell.

Shanna might suspect my near slip of the tongue, because she looks smugly pleased.

"Over here!" Stacy calls, waving to us with a lot of enthusiasm. At least *someone* at this table's happy to see me. The restaurant is very high-end Thai, the kind with waterfalls running along fake rocks, bamboo wind chimes, and Buddhas sitting on golden lotus leaves. The table's long, with most of the people we met last night chatting together.

Shanna and I sit down next to each other, and I'm doing everything but clutching her hand under the table. I didn't just bring Shanna along to sample Nate's largesse —*heh. Large. Stop it*—I'm bringing her along to act as something of a human shield. Because now that I've started really remembering last night's encounter in the closet, I find that I'm . . . kind of excited to see him again. A little nervous as well.

Basically, I want someone familiar sitting next to me, someone to keep me grounded. Something that'll stop me from lying on top of the table screaming, "Do me now, again, harder."

That kind of thing can put people off their Panang curry.

"Julia, look. Sit down over here," Stacy says, patting a chair right next to her. "I want to talk a little more about your books."

Sure she does. Because sitting right on the other side of this chair is Nate, studiously avoiding my gaze. I hope he's memorizing that menu, because he barely looks up from it. I already know it wasn't his idea to bring me; my stomach sinks a little at the thought. I get the feeling Stacy is good at getting what she wants. Shanna gives me a wink.

"Go ahead. Sit with the bride," she says, flashing me a smile. Ugh. Traitorous friend. *Et tu*, Shanna? With no one else to turn to, I walk around the table to take my seat.

"Hey stranger," I say to Nate, keeping my voice light and bright. He finally tears his eyes away from the Thai peanut chicken lunch special. Good. I know how riveting it must have been.

"Hey," he says, gazing at me. An involuntary thrill runs up my spine. Why didn't I ever notice how sexy his voice is? It's like baritone scotch, rich and smoky. His eyes, still that perfect dark blue, seem to pierce me.

Heh. Pierce.

Shut up, David Tennant.

I'm out of my mind. I clutch my napkin, determined to keep my raging hormones under control. But I can't help how my eyes travel down his body, remembering the silk and steel feeling of him beneath my hands, and I imagine him naked. Despite how, er, intimately we know each other, so much of him is still a mystery. Didn't see much in all of our action last night—at least, not that I can remember. I want to see him laid out under soft lighting, maybe in that lush hotel bed from last night. And while we're dreaming, maybe I'm on top, riding him, taking him between my . . . .

"Are you drooling?" Nate sounds kind of mortified.

"Nothing. Er, the medication," I lie, wanting to slam my own head against the table. I discreetly wipe my mouth. "My medication, for. Stuff."

Shut up, Julia.

He hands me the menu.

"See what you like," he says.

Oh, I think I do see something I like, you magnificent, arrogant jerkface.

I am not using my grown-up words today. Instead, I look over the menu and finally settle on some chicken satay skewers. I'm not that hungry. I ran out on a mostly eaten club sandwich and salad back at the hotel restaurant.

Now there's nothing for Nate and me to do but . . . talk. Stacy, for all her pretense of wanting some girl chat, is talking with Mike and Shanna about something.

Stacy. You tricksy little hobbit.

"You made it back to the hotel okay?" I ask Nate, taking a sip of ice water. Ice. Ice is good. Ice cools down the throbbing libido.

"No, I was stranded. Left alone to fend for myself in the desert," he says, his voice so cool and under control I nearly take him seriously. This man has an expert poker face. "So I opened up this restaurant, built it with my own two hands. At least now we can get quality Thai in the desert," he says.

I laugh, and the lines around his mouth and eyes ease. He never seemed to like my laugh before. But then again, I never used to fantasize about him fucking me senseless, so there you have it. His sarcasm doesn't bother me. Well, not as much as it did yesterday afternoon.

Sometimes you have to get to know people. Even if it's biblically.

Nate pulls out his phone, buzzing in his pocket. He frowns.

"Shit. Work. Excuse me," Nate says, pulling out his chair and getting up. He heads off, probably to go stand outside. Stacy winks at me.

"You two had fun last night," she says.

Would it be really wrong to grab her, shake her, and scream, *"Tell me what we did because I remember almost nothing except doing a stripper dance and then fucking in a closet with a neon condom*"? I think it would be wrong.

"I'm glad you guys have been, y'know, seeing so much of each other."

Oh hardy har.

"Nate's been a grouch for too long."

"He was ever a not-grouch?" I ask. I'm trying not to sound as intrigued as I feel. The food arrives, and Stacy twirls some pad thai onto her fork. "I mean, you must've known him way young."

"Pretty much. We all went to college together. Northwestern. Go Wildcats." She grins. Oh man, I went to University of Wisconsin. We can discuss Big Ten rivalries later. "We graduated a decade ago, we were all friends since sophomore year. And I'm only now getting this one to commit," she says, grinning across the table at Mike. He puts a hand over his chest, mock-wounded.

"I just wanted to wait until we could afford a condo. Was that a crime?"

Condos. Joking with each other over lunch. For the first time in a while, I feel lonely for Drew. Jerk though he was, he used to be my jerk.

"You know how he finally bought the ring and proposed?" Stacy asks me. Uh, is this a pop quiz? "Nate," she says, answering her own question.

"Get out. Mr. Love Is a Battlefield? Mr. Grumpy Cat transformed into a human being? I'm surprised he didn't hiss and turn into a pile of ashes when you showed him the ring."

Nate tried to *help* his friends' relationship? Nate the great divorce attorney was pushing for his friends to get *married*?

"He made Mike get the ring, haggled with the jeweler until he took down the price. Then he and Mike talked about where to take me to propose, everything. They decided on Wrigley Field, the very minute the Cubs lost. He knew it would cheer me up." She smiles. "Nate pays attention to the people he cares about. He's a genuinely good guy. I'll admit, you didn't see the best of him yesterday afternoon." Stacy sighs. "Sometimes he can be a real asshole. I love him, and even I know it."

"So does being an asshole just come with the lawyerly territory?" I ask.

Stacy smiles, but only a little. "He's not usually this bad. I know he's doing his best with this wedding, being the best man. But the love thing, seeing us celebrate it all weekend; I know it's taking a toll on him." She looks sad.

"What happened?" I ask. I smell a tragic back story. Actually, my stomach tightens just thinking about it. Is it bad that I'm curious?

"His girlfriend, Phoebe. She was almost his fiancée. Mike tells me Nate had his own ring, his own perfect spot to propose picked out. They're both lawyers, met at U Chicago law school. Both really smart, really type A. It seemed like a match made in heaven." Stacy shrugs. "And then she dumped him. Out of the blue. She told him on a Friday afternoon that it was over, packed her shit and headed out Saturday morning. There was a moving van waiting and everything when Nate woke up. She'd planned the whole thing. She was gone in twenty-four hours. I'd never seen Nate surprised before. Or crushed." She sighs. "I didn't like seeing it. He hid it fast, but those first few days." She shakes her head.

"Jesus," I whisper. "When did this happen?"

"Six months ago," she says.

Holy shit. That wound's probably still fresh, especially at a wedding. No wonder he's been so pissed off.

"Then Nate kind of turned into robot lawyer man, and we couldn't get him to even mention Phoebe's name. He never talks about it, but I know it's been eating at him." She crunches a peanut.

"Why did she leave him? Do you know?" I ask, feeling that familiar knot in my stomach. Boy, do I know what it's like to have abandonment issues. "There has to be a reason."

"This was the part that really got to him. Phoebe told him she had finally met her soul mate. It was total serendipity. He was just some guy who lent her his coat at Wrigley Field one night. She told Nate the second she looked into this other guy's eyes, she knew it was meant to be." Stacy says it all with kind of a sarcastic bite, but I'm not so quick to make fun.

Isn't that what I write about for a living? Two strangers meeting across a crowded room, or at a corporate meeting? Or—if I'm feeling kinky enough—in a Hungarian sex dungeon? Whatever the venue, I love to write about that moment of connection, eyes meeting, pulses elevating. That instant when you spy in someone else the missing piece of your soul.

Hell, how many times have I written the plotline of "she's engaged to marry some bland doofus and ends up running off with her hot sports manager/corporate tycoon/rock star soul mate"? Normally, those "doofuses" are only guilty of not being the heroine's perfect match. They're usually sweet, kind, Bill Pullman in *Sleepless in Seattle* types. Why don't I ever write what happens to those people after they're dumped?

Why don't I talk about their quest to find love again, when they've been so thoroughly shafted?

I really need to think about the damage I inflict on fictional people.

"I guess this puts things in a whole new light," I say softly.

"Give him a chance to get better. Hey, even if it's just a fun fling in Vegas, I think it'll be good for you both." Stacy takes a sip of her Mai Tai. "He's a real catch. When we were in college, I had a crush on Nate before Mike. Don't tell him that."

"What about hot college Nate?" Mike asks, ears perking up like a fox whose fiancée is hitting on someone else.

"What about still-hot me?" Nate asks, sitting down, putting his phone back in his pocket.

While Stacy and Mike banter some more, I clear my throat. Maybe it's the writer in me, but now that I'm imagining Nate as the stoic, alpha lawyer whose heart was shattered and who can never love again, I'm finding a way to relate to him better.

"We were just talking about . . . stuff," I say at last. Brilliant.

Nate smiles. "Stuff's very interesting." He leans a little closer to whisper in my ear. My pulse elevates, but it's pure business talk. "So. You didn't figure out anything else? In terms of what felonies we committed last night, that is," he says.

I try to grin, but it's more of a tight wince. Why the hell am I so nervous around him?

"I'm pretty sure that if our crimes were anything mafia-related, we'd have been taken down by now and stuffed into the trunk of a car. And the yakuza don't tend to frequent Vegas in the off season," I say.

Nate shrugs. "I always admire a woman who's up to date on the movements of Japanese organized crime."

"Great. It's one of my favorite subjects," I say, getting a Mai Tai of my own. Why the hell not? Vegas, baby. "You never found my purse, did you?" I ask.

Nate sighs. "I searched every inch of that strip club. The guys let me in early. And by the way, you don't want to crawl around on those floors," he says, shuddering.

"You risked stripper gunk and dried jizz to find my purse?" I clasp my hands between my breasts. "You, sir, are my valiant hero."

"Why did you have to bring up jizz when we're about to eat?" he grumbles. But this time, he doesn't sound so annoyed. In fact, he smiles.

"I'm all about shaving off calories when I can," I say primly, dunking my chicken satay in the peanut dipping sauce. "Watching the Donald Trump campaign, for example. Great way for a three-day fast."

"Oh God. I was so hungry," he says, sounding pained and wincing over his food. "And now I don't think I'll eat again."

"I'll shut up," I say.

"No, it's all right. It's nice hearing you talk," he says, taking a mouthful of green curry. "You're . . . funny."

A compliment from Nate Wexler? I nearly faint.

"Sweeter words were never spoken," I say lightly. But I can't help studying the way his throat works as he swallows. He smells good, too, like chlorine and sun, and some rich, musky cologne. It kind of makes me hungry.

Chicken satay, work your dark magic to prevent my horniness from overpowering me.

We get through lunch, and I don't want to murder Nate, and he doesn't complain about what a pain in the ass I am. In fact, we share some laughs and stories from his college days. Far as I'm concerned, we're a massive success. We pay the check, and then all head out to grab a cab.

Damn, I didn't realize Mike and Stacy were getting married today. They've got a busy few hours ahead of them. Shanna and Tyler are still talking—he seems to be into her, though it could be because she's a cute girl with a pulse—and Mike and Stacy have their arms around each other. Young love is a beautiful thing to witness.

"They look happy," Nate says. Even he sounds gruffly pleased for them. "At least someone is." His gaze darkens as he says it. He squares his jaw just a bit.

Pure rejected alpha pain, right here on display.

Should I bring up the *I know your tragic back story* angle? No, maybe not. Right now, we've just entered the realm of civility.

Stacy reaches into her enormous tote bag for something. She stops talking to Mike, fishes around, and then comes up with—

"Holy shit," Stacy cries, pulling out my purse. It is definitely mine; hard to find a vinyl number in that particular shade of hot pink. Her eyes go wide. "I forgot I had this. I found it in the boys' hotel suite this morning, and you weren't there, and—shit. I was going to find you after breakfast, but everything started happening and . . . . I'm so sorry. You must've been frantic," she says, turning back to me.

I practically tear it out of her hands. I check my important things, and they're all there. Credit cards, driver's license, everything.

"I didn't know how I was going to get on the plane without my ID." I groan, squeezing the damn purse to my chest. "I love you, Stacy. Long time. Very long time."

"Careful now, it's my wedding day." Stacy laughs. I turn back to Nate, who's eyeing my purse with curiosity.

"You think there's anything in there? Related to what we did last night?" he asks.

Oh shit. Maybe.

"You coming?" Stacy calls, grinning widely at us as they all cram into a cab. I smile and shrug.

"We'll, ah, catch up with you all back at the hotel."

"Have fun," Shanna calls, wiggling her eyebrows.

Yep. We'll have a ton of fun tracking down whatever insane shit we did last night. A regular Nick and Nora Charles, that's us. Except without the insane amount of drinking and the murder mystery. Well. Without one of those things. Hopefully.

While the taxi drives away, we dig through my purse. At first we find only the normal stuff, wallet, lip gloss. At least I don't have to carry my iPhone in my pocket any longer. I dump it in with the other items.

"What's this?" Nate asks, finally noticing my phone and its blue, British telephone box casing.

"The TARDIS. Remember, like the one on my ass now?" I grumble. "If only you were a Whovian," I tell him, continuing to paw through my things.

"A whatvian?"

"Who, not what. I mentioned it before, it's a show—"
And then I stop dead. Because in my hand, there's a ball
of gauzy white fabric.

Nate furrows his brow and grabs it, holds it up like
he's examining it.

"Why do you have Stacy's bridal veil?" he asks,
puzzling over it. But my heart's now wedged right in my
throat. That makes breathing kind of awkward.

"Stacy's veil was shorter. And had a tiara. Trust me,
romance authors know one wedding veil from the other."

Is it just me, or is the desert rippling in front of my
eyes right now? I expect a mirage any second, a neon sign
with flashing lights shimmering, spelling out YOU'RE
SCREWED in bold lettering.

"So whose is it?" Nate asks. He's sounding a little
panicked as well; I think he's putting two and two
together.

"Hang on." I turn on my phone and flip through my
photos. I don't know why I didn't think to do this before,
but I don't have to look very far.

There we are, sloppily drunk and grinning, with our
arms around each other. My veil is hanging kind of askew
on my head, and my lipstick is smeared all the way down
my cheek. And all over Nate's face as well. But there's no
mistaking the Elvis Presley impersonator standing behind
us, holding up two gold wedding rings and grinning that
lopsided King grin.

It can't. It can't be.

"Did we get . . . " Nate chokes on the last word, then
manages it. "Married?"

We gaze into each other's eyes, horror seeming to
flood both of us at the exact same time. Good thing, too,

because if one was super excited and the other was about to vomit all over everything, it'd be kind of awkward.

"What do we do now?" I whisper.

"We need to stay calm." He switches right into Lawyer Mode™ and puts his hands on my shoulders. Like I'm the one who needs to be soothed right now. "Do you remember what chapel it was?"

Before I can answer that, a white van pulls up directly in front of us, sending a cloud of dust swirling into the air. We both blink at it, neither knowing what to do when the door slides open and three guys in black balaclavas jump out.

Yes. Three guys in balaclavas. I don't believe it at first, either.

Between the face coverings and the all black clothing, for a second I think a ninja dance party is going to break out. Until one of them rolls across the sand, distracting us, and the other two grab us. One guy pins my arms to my sides, the other seems to put Nate in a headlock. I cry out in horror, kicking backwards, but it's no use. They drag me toward the van. I start screaming, but a thick, beefy hand covers my mouth.

"What the fuck?" Nate shouts. One of the men walks up to us, his eyes—the only thing I can see of his face— narrowed and calculating.

"You're coming with us, meester!" he hisses in a thick Russian accent. Then a bag goes over my head, and the sunlit desert gets turned out like a light.

In conclusion: *Fuck Vegas. Fuck fuck fuck fuck fuck Vegas in its glittery ass.*

13

NATE

I NEED TO STAY CALM.

Those five words keep repeating over and over in my mind. Julia isn't shrieking about this any longer, so the quiet has helped me think. I had no idea what lung power she had. There was a good five minutes after they first put us into the van where she screamed something about sparkling ball sacks and dildos without Vaseline shoved into sensitive areas. While I'm not sure I appreciate the imagery, I know she has spirit. I admire that, but she should have realized when the fight became hopeless. As soon as they had us bound, I knew there was no way, in that moment, to fight back. Not without my hands free and my eyes uncovered.

This isn't to say I'm giving up. Far from it. It just became very clear very quickly that I either wait until they pull the sacks off our heads—by which time it may be too late—or I manage to slip out of my bonds. And since my hands are tied with rope, not handcuffs or plastic zips, I think I have a solid chance.

While I test the knots, I keep asking myself: *What did you do, asshole? What did you do last night to cause this?*

Around me, the men keep speaking in very, very thick Russian accents.

Shit. If they're working for the Russian mafia, the police will never find our bodies.

No, fuck asking what *I* did. What did Julia do last night? Steal their money? Crash their car? Punch one of them in the face? Because I know I would never be drunk enough to get into trouble with the goddamn Russian mob. Even I'm not that much of an idiot.

Julia, though? She's spirited as hell, but that can be a serious problem sometimes.

"You, fancy man." I think the goon is talking to me. "Take woman. She kick," the asshole says, and sits Julia on my lap.

"I'll kick like a mule, you Moscow piece of shit," she snaps. After a minute, "Get it? Moscow mule?" She laughs; no one else does. "Christ I could use a drink about now."

"Maybe shut up for a while," I whisper in her ear. I can't see her—that seems to be a continuing theme in our quasi relationship—but I can feel her. Her round, perfect ass is pressed up right against me, hardening my dick.

Fuck, I'm about to get my head blasted off by Russian mobsters, and it's all I can do to keep my erection from—

"I just wanted to tell you," Julia mutters. "You've either got the barrel of a gun clamped between your legs, or you're very happy to see me."

"Hilarious," I say.

"Personally, I'd be very happy to see the barrel of a gun right now, at least one that's on our side, so I can't fault you there." She sounds a little high-pitched. She's probably freaking the fuck out. And why shouldn't she?

"Out of curiosity, did we cross any mobsters last night?" I ask.

"Right after the strip club fucking, right before the skinny dipping, and maybe sandwiched in the middle of our blackout drunk quickie wedding? Gee, let me check my calendar, I'm sure I'll find it wedged right in there," Julia snaps.

I give her a little bounce on my knee. That's sexier than I thought it would be and . . . fuck, I'm hard again.

"You two are strangest hostages we ever have," one of the mobsters says.

"Where the fuck are you taking us?" I snap. The guy says nothing, but, wonder of wonders, I start to work a hand free. Fuck me, yes. It's not much, but if I need to, I can untie myself.

For the moment, I sit tight. This is the one element of surprise I have, and I'll be damned if I give it up too soon.

Julia lies back against me, her head finally cradled against my shoulder. "I suppose we should be a little more helpful to each other right now," she says.

Helpful's good. Helpful will probably not get us killed. Her lying against me now, it's comforting. I shouldn't have been thinking about how she clearly must have made this happen. I don't remember much of last night any better than she does. Apparently I can be incredibly impulsive when I have a few too many drinks in me.

"I'm sorry I implied this was all your fault," I mutter. "For all we know, I'm the one who landed us in this situation."

"Thanks, Mr. Wexler. Nice to know you're not a complete dick," she drawls.

Give some people an inch, man.

We ride in silence, until, finally, the van stops. My heart starts pounding, adrenaline coursing through my veins. This is it. I hope to God they take the hoods off, because otherwise this is going to be fucking impossible.

I hear the van door slide open, and two of the men talk to each other. Julia is pulled out of my lap. She gives a yelp, like she's in pain, and instantly I want to rip people's heads off. I rise to my feet, banging my head on top of the van roof. Cursing, I snarl at them.

"Where are you taking her? Are you all right? Julia?" I call. She doesn't answer. Oh, shit. "Julia?"

"Calm down, hero man. We take you see her now," one of the men says, strong-arming me out of the van.

I'm tempted to pull right out of my fucking ropes and give them a surprise, but not yet.

Wait. You'll know when the moment presents itself, Wexler.

My feet hit the ground, and I can feel the sun on my back. The men shove me forward at least ten paces until they finally force me to stop. Then one of these jackasses rips the sack from off my head, and I'm left blinking in the light.

Around us, there's only desert. Red mountains in the distance bake in the hot sunlight. The highway that stretches before us is dead. We're alone. The wind whistles by, and it's so quiet I can hear the blood working in my ears.

Julia's standing right next to me, her blue eyes the widest I've seen them. That's pretty damn wide. She glances over at me.

"Did they hurt you?" I ask her. It comes out as more of a growl. Despite the playing it cool game, if any of these fuckers tried anything—

"I'm awesome. As always," she says, scanning the four —no, five—balaclava-wearing assholes surrounding us.

Impressive. With her purple lace bras and *Doctor Who* phones, at first I'd have pegged Julia as the type to curl up into a ball and plead for mercy from these scumbags. Instead, she's facing them down with a look of steely resolve. I like a woman with backbone, and I've never seen more nerve than this.

I don't need another hard-on right now.

"All right," the biggest, burliest masked asshole says. He takes out a Glock and points it at us. "What you have to say for yourselves?"

Now is not the time to freeze. My heart pounding in my throat, I feel the last tightness in the ropes around my wrists falling away. So close. If I can get the gun away from him . . . . It's not impossible. Just another minute . . . .

"Let's start with, what the hell are we doing out here, you crazy pieces of shit?" Julia snaps. She actually stomps her foot.

Christ. Keep calm. Don't antagonize the man with the fucking gun.

The Russian human tank laughs. I mean he guffaws, actually tilting his head back towards the sky. Overconfident ass. "Puny woman think we crazy," he tells his friends, who start laughing and knee-slapping right along. Good. Show contempt for your hostages. "But perhaps it is puny woman who go crazy. When my men and I each take a turn."

Fuck. Every hair on my body raises up. The adrenaline is making the corners of my vision turn sharp and bright.

I will make you eat that gun, motherfucker. I need a minute to prepare, let the rope fall, and then—

"Fuck you!" Julia screams. She dashes forward, hands still tied behind her back, and stomps her wedge sandaled heel hard onto the asshole's foot. She gets him right in the instep, a confident move. He curses, but before he can blast her she high kicks straight into his crotch. The guy's eyes seem to bug right out of his sockets, and . . . he drops the gun.

Julia, you crazy fucking genius.

"Girl loose," one of the thugs shouts. It's the one standing right next to me, and I turn around, my hands now free.

"She is," I say, in full agreement. Then I punch the dickhead right in the face. My knuckles immediately explode in pain, and I swear I feel blood running down my fingers, but hopefully nothing is broken. I duck and dodge the attackers, rolling in the dirt to grab the gun while Julia continues kicking the shit out of the biggest guy's side.

There I am, with a gun in my hands. It's like I snap back to sanity. What the fuck am I doing? I don't even know how to use one of these goddamn things.

"Hold it on him!" Julia shouts, dodging around the guy and circling back behind me. She grunts as she struggles to get out of the rope tied around her wrists. So I hold up the damn gun and aim it at the mobster's chest.

"Don't fucking move," I tell the guy on the ground. "Now. What the hell is going on?"

The dude sits up, groaning and rubbing his head. Then he says, in a perfectly normal American accent, "The fuck is wrong with you people? Jesus, I think I got a lump the size of a goddamn egg." He moans and winces as he touches the side of his scalp. He then glares up at Julia and me. "You maniacs shouldn't be allowed to drive a car, let alone hire people for role play!"

"Hold on," I say, blinking rapidly and bringing down the gun. "We hired you? Role play? What?"

Have I lost what precious little of my mind I still have?

"Are you kidding me with this?" the guy says, looking over to the others in amazement.

I watch as they each pull their balaclavas off, shooting Julia and me sullen, dirty looks. They seem like completely normal guys, with patchy beards, pale skin, and slight double chins. It's like the cast of *The Office* suddenly decided to go into the kidnapping business.

"What are you talking about?" I repeat, still stunned.

"Check out your gun, genius," the guy on the ground snaps. "That thing look real to you?"

Now that he mentions it, the gun does feel a little lightweight. I point it away, and pull the trigger. Nothing. A few plastic clicks. Christ, it's a toy.

"I'm sorry, I'm still not following. We hired you to do what exactly?" Julia snaps. One of the guys comes forward with a piece of paper.

"We're an adventure role-play company. You know?" He rolls his eyes. "Your own Indiana Jones adventure? Actually, you didn't want the treasure cave adventure; you guys chose the kidnapping and desert escape. Remember?" Our obliviousness makes this guy snort.

"Jesus, you guys came into our office at like, one in the morning."

"You're open at one?" I say, incredulous.

The guy shrugs. "Some people like nighttime adventures. You know, night vision goggles and shit? Anyway, you came in and ordered a deluxe package for this afternoon. Remember? We added our stalker app to your phone just to know where you'd be so we could show up when you least expected. Holy shit, you don't remember any of this?" The guy sounds disgusted. "How drunk were you two?"

The guy hands over the sheet of paper. The guy I punched is rubbing his nose, and I think he might be crying. Shit. This could be a lawsuit.

Julia takes the paper first, looks it over, then passes it to me with an expression that can only be described as nauseated and bemused. "Check it out," she says.

I look and, yep, that's my credit card number. Fucking fantastic.

"We were really bombed last night," Julia tells the man by way of apology as he snatches the paper back. "Like, really bombed. Actually, do you happen to remember where we went after we left your office? Were you there?"

"You people are insane," the man snaps.

Well, no argument there.

He whistles, and the other men jump back into the van. He gets into the front seat while the driver guns the engine. The van door slams shut.

Oh, fuck me.

"Hold on, you can't leave us out here. It's the middle of nowhere!" I shout as I run to the van and start banging on the side.

The tires squeal, and I jump out of the way just in time to watch the van tear back onto the highway, kicking up gravel in its wake. A cloud of dust engulfs me, and I cough and wipe my eyes. When the cloud clears, the van is driving fast down the highway, getting smaller by the second.

Now we're alone. Me, Julia, her impractical wedge sandals, and . . . yep. I hold up my phone and walk around. Zero bars on my cell. It takes all my self-control to keep from throwing the damn phone to the ground and jumping up and down on it.

"This," I say, stalking to the side of the road, my teeth gritted, "could have been handled better."

"My, how observant you are," Julia deadpans. She groans and picks up her left foot. "Great, I think I'm getting a blister."

"I'm going to have their asses in a sling," I mutter, starting to walk toward town. At least, I hope to God this is toward town. "Litigation wise, that is."

"Yeah, I think they could maybe charge us with assault. Not that I'm a lawyer or anything," Julia says, slinging her purse up to her shoulder and hiking along- side me. She coughs as a cloud of dust washes over us, and she spits a piece of hair out of her mouth.

Even watching that is starting to turn me on.

I'm losing my mind.

"What now?" she asks, and we halt to let a tumble- weed pass. A goddamn tumbleweed. I swear, if this turns into some animated cartoon with comically placed buffalo skulls and vultures circling overhead . . . .

"Now we walk," I say. Julia nods.

"Sounds about right."

We tromp along, side by side. She puts her arm through mine as we trudge along, and I don't say anything. As bullshit as this whole day has been, her arm in mine feels sort of nice.

14

JULIA

TWO MILES LATER, my shoes are dangling in my hand, the back of my heel is rubbed raw, the rocks are hurting my feet, and I'm probably married to Nate Wexler.

Of all these things, I'm not sure which is the most uncomfortable.

"We didn't even sign a pre-nup," I tell him. He flinches, and I'm surprised his hand doesn't instantly fly to his wallet. "Relax. I've got enough money. I don't need to hit you up for anything."

"Let's focus on not dying in the desert, and afterwards I'll walk you through all the delights of divorce litigation," he tells me. His temples are slick with sweat, and he stumbles a little bit on a rock.

Uh oh. If he goes down, there's no way I'll be able to drag him. I mean, it'd be hilarious, but impossible.

Or maybe I could just stretch him out on the side of the road and give in to the passion one last time before our inevitable deserty death.

Man. Getting stranded makes you morbid and inappropriately horny.

"We might not really be married," I say.

"We might not. But as Sherlock Holmes said, once you eliminate the impossible, whatever remains, however improbable, must be the truth." Nate sighs.

I smile. "I should've pegged you for a Holmesian. Logic, aloofness, doing whatever your friends need even though you pretend like you don't have human emotions." I sigh playfully. "I'm surprised you don't have a deerstalker hat. Now *that* would've been a fun role play. Sherlock Holmes was probably dynamite in bed."

"Oh, I guarantee it," he says, gazing right into my eyes. His gaze is hypnotic, electric, even at the most inopportune times. I think he means to be funny, but it doesn't feel like that.

"Well, Benedict Cumberbatch is my favorite Holmes, so I'm right with you there." I laugh, a little breathless. Though maybe the breathless part is because we're hiking in a damn desert without water.

We're silent for a bit, and all I can think of is, holy shit. I might be married to this guy. Mom will flip out. She'll say it's too fast for me to be married to someone else. Then she'll make a Velveeta and macaroni dish, sit Nate down on the couch, and show him all the family pictures I managed to upload to iPhoto for her. She'll tell him every single detail of every single member of our family. Hope Nate likes seeing my grandpa's Illinois neighborhood back in the Great Depression, and the luau our Hoboken branch of the family threw in the 70s. Grass skirts, coconut bras, the works.

All kidding aside, this is pretty fucking serious.

"That was kind of a stupid move back there," Nate says. At first I think he's talking about himself, but then I notice he's fixed me with a particularly irritated gaze. So I pull us to a quick stop.

"Excuse me? I wasn't the one who grabbed a gun and started waving it around without a clue of how to use it," I say, slipping my arm out of his.

"I wouldn't have had to do anything that drastic if you hadn't stomped on that man's foot. And then kicked him in the balls. And then in the side." Nate wipes his forehead; he's red-faced, sweaty, and looking for someone to blame. "They would've given us a ride back to town if you hadn't—"

"Pulled a gun on them and threatened to shoot?" I ask, really drawing the words out. Nate pauses. *Yeah, that's right, Wexler. Gun trumps nut kick.* "For all we knew, we were in real trouble. I had to do something, didn't I?"

"That something would've gotten you killed if it hadn't been pretend," he snaps. "Doesn't that matter?"

"Maybe I wouldn't have had to go *Death Wish* on those assholes if you'd done something yourself." I cross my arms. "Yeah, you probably had your hands loose a while before, and you didn't do shit."

"I was thinking about how to react," he says with that maddening magna cum laude tone of his. "If you don't think, you're no better than an animal."

"And if you don't react when you're threatened, or someone you care about is threatened, you're no better than a computer!" I yell.

Nate tilts his head. "Someone you care about?" he echoes.

Oh, shit. My cheeks are flushed solely because of the desert. That's it.

"Hypothetically. Isn't that a word you lawyers love? You're all crazy about hypothetical bullshit," I grumble, and stomp ahead. I don't recommend stomping on hot sand and rocks in your bare feet, but dammit, this moment called for a stomp.

Nate sighs. "Come back," he says.

"Save your apologies," I call behind me. I hear his footsteps crunching behind me, catching up. Well, when he does, we can have a good talk—

I'm swept off my feet. Literally. Nate grunts, but hefts me into his arms and walks.

"What are you doing?" I say.

"The ground's hurting your feet," Nate says. He shrugs, a little difficult while carrying me. "I wanted to give you a rest for a bit."

"I can walk," I say, though it's a little sullen. Nate grins.

"I know. But I wanted to be a gentleman about it."

This guy. Can anyone figure this guy out? One minute he's lecturing me, the next he's pulling a John Wayne and carrying me out of the desert. It's kind of exasperating. Maybe a little sexy, too.

"Well. Let me know if you get tired," I say. He's moving pretty well, though. Must work out. I mean, if his body looks like it felt last night, he must work out a lot.

"I'll put you back down when we reach that mirage right in front of us," he grumbles.

I look ahead. I see it. Damn, it's a good mirage, too. It's a squat white and blue painted building rippling ahead in the desert heat. A wooden sign has a picture of a cherry pie on it, and letters that spell out the word DINER on top of that . . . .

Wait a minute. No mirage is that detailed.

"On second thought," Nate says, relief flooding his voice. "I think we're saved."

I'm not even listening now; I scramble out of his arms, shoes still clutched in my hand, and charge over to the building. I don't even feel the hot sand and rocks on my feet any longer. Whoever decided to build a diner along a desolate stretch of highway in the middle of Nevadan nowhere gets my unadulterated love forever and ever.

I pull open the door, a bell tinkling overhead, and a blast of perfect, air-conditioned air hits me.

"Yo! No shoes, no service," the man behind the counter yells. He's got a craggy face and an even craggier personality.

Whatever. I abide by your rules, slinger of pie and refreshments. As I tug my sandals back on, Nate comes up beside me.

"Treat you to a glass of water?" he asks. He seems as relieved as I feel.

"Love one." We walk in and slide into a red vinyl booth. The seat is cracked and stuffing is sticking out of it, but right now it's the sweetest sight ever.

The craggy guy brings us each a glass of water, and we suck them down. I even pick up an ice cube and run it over my forehead, luxuriating in the icy perfection of it all.

"Feeling better?" Nate asks, leaning back in his seat. He's definitely sweaty, the dampness of his shirt accentuating the perfect lines of his torso. I don't mind.

"Maybe we should get some pie to celebrate?" I ask.

"I can't have too many sweet things in the day," he says, closing his eyes in relief. "It interferes with the metabolism."

"You drink kale smoothies?" I ask. "With lemon juice?"

"No." He makes a pained expression. "I'm just careful with what I eat."

"Probably a good thing if we're not married," I say, shrugging. "For me, a little sugar in the day is the way of life. There's supposed to be this all jelly bean store somewhere in Vegas that I've been dying to go to."

"I'm shuddering just thinking about it," he says. He pulls out his phone, checks it, and smiles. "Full bars. All right. Be right back, and then I'll call a cab." He puts the phone on the table and gets up.

"First nature calls, then you?" I grin at him.

"Thanks for phrasing it in such a delicate fashion," he says. But I think he sounds amused.

"It's what I'm here for."

He walks away, and I run another ice cube down my forehead, along my cheek, riiiight into my cleavage. It's necessary. What can I tell you? A man that cold is also very hot.

Okay. Enough with the temperature jokes.

Nate's phone rings, and I jump in my seat a little. Then I frown. Who the hell set his ring tone to "Blame Canada" from *South Park*? Weird choice.

Oh wait, shit. I did that. I remember now. My bad.

I grab the call without even thinking.

Well, actually, that's a lie. I have been thinking. And when I see the caller ID—Phoebe Barnes—I instinctively jump all over that shit. This has to be *the* Phoebe, the one who stomped on his heart and paraded off into the sunset with her soul mate.

"Hello?" I say when I answer, already feeling like an idiot who didn't think this through.

"Who the hell is this?" a woman shouts.

I wince and hold the phone away from my ear. Man, I really thought a guy like Nate would be into classier women.

Then again, he had spent a wild night with me.

Yeah, I probably don't want to fling too many insults around at women Nate's slept with.

"This is—uh, ah, uhm. How can I help you?"

"Where's Nate?" she snaps.

Man, it sounds like something crawled straight up this woman's ass.

"In the bathroom. Uh. How are you?" I wince.

Great job, loser.

"I know he's in Las Vegas. And now I can't find Peebles. Do you think that's a coincidence?" the woman screams, her voice rising higher and higher.

Wow. You could shatter glass at this pitch.

"Let's start with the basics. What is a Peebles?" I ask.

"Tell that asshole to call me back!" Phoebe shouts, and the line goes dead.

Good. Remind me never to pick up on a one-night stand's crazy ex. Especially when I might be married to said one-night stand.

When Nate returns, I hand him the phone. "You, ah, need to call Phoebe back," I tell him.

His face kind of goes slack, and my stomach does a small swan dive. That's the kind of face you make when someone you still have a thing for gets in touch for mysterious reasons. Trust me, I know that look well. I had to stand in the mirror for hours in the months after my separation from Drew, training my facial muscles not to do that.

"Did she say what she wanted?" he asks.

I'm sure he wishes that she did nothing but coo sweet nothings and weep bitter tears of heartbreak. Instead, I have to go with the truth.

"She screamed obscenities and asked if I knew where Peebles was. Is Peebles, like, some kind of rare artifact or something?"

Nate looks as astonished as I feel. "Peebles. Holy shit," he says, his eyes adopting a kind of weird light.

"Am I supposed to guess, or?"

"Peebles is Phoebe's special gray spotted Tibetan parrot," he explains, rubbing his hand across his sexy, gradually becoming stubbled jaw.

Man, he shouldn't shave. This is a good look on him.

Fuck it, pay attention. We were talking about parrots. As you do in Vegas.

"So Phoebe lives in Vegas with Peebles and her fiancé. And this has what to do with us?" I ask.

"Don't you remember last night?" he asks, looking incredibly grave.

I'm about to make an obvious comment, when a flash goes off in my mind. A flash of squawking gray feathers and hushed giggling.

We exchange an incredulous look, the memory apparently rushing back to us at the exact same time.

"Oh, shit," I moan.

15

NATE

"YOU KNOW what I need after a good workout?" Julia asks me as she licks salt suggestively from off her hand. "More alcohol. It does a body good."

She giggles and tosses her hair. I lean over and kiss her neck. She groans softly as I slide my hand up her knee, skimming the silky line of her thigh. This may be a dive bar, with a juke box blasting Johnny Cash and the crack of pool balls in the background, but right now Julia Stevens is all that exists for me.

I can't remember how we got here. When did we lose Mike and the others? I should be more worried about it than I am, but my hand slides further up Julia's thigh, right into the danger zone. *Fuck yeah, Kenny Loggins.*

"You two need to get a hotel if you're gonna do that," the bartender grumbles, pouring us two more shots of tequila. He's an old man with eyes like a desert hawk and a moustache like Yosemite Sam if he stuck his finger in an electrical socket. "I don't care if this is the Strip, this place is respectable."

"Respectable me, then," I say, dimly aware it makes no sense.

Hmm. I might be drunk.

I can't remember what bar this is. I just remember a sign that had a neon cowboy throwing a lasso around a woman's leg, and I thought, *That's where I need to be.*

The old guy's not giving up, though. Julia moans a little in disappointment as I remove my hand. Gotta respect the man's wishes. He moves away, finally.

"Relax." I nibble at her exposed shoulder. "Plenty of time later."

"You've got great stamina." She winks at me. "Much better than my ex. He used to be only up for twice in one night. And the second time would always be too quick." She huffs and bites into a lime wedge.

"Fucker didn't know what he had," I whisper, pulling her against me and kissing her. She tastes like lime and tequila; a potent combination. Her lips part, and I flick my tongue inside her mouth. Her groan makes me rise to half-mast.

Down, boy.

"He especially didn't like it when I started making more money than him." She sighs and pulls away, leaning her cheek against her hand. "Romance writing was fun and sexy when I was doing it on my own, making five hundred bucks every six weeks on Amazon. He liked it 'cause he got to work as my 'research,' and we got enough extra cash for nice dinners a couple times a month. He was fine with that part. But as soon as my agent picked me up, and my career took off? As soon as I was pulling in contracts worth a couple hundred thousand? Bye." She throws back another tequila shot. "Suddenly I was a workaholic bitch who didn't give him blowjobs anymore. And I did!" she cries, slamming her shot glass onto the bar. "I gave him plenty of blowjobs! I'm a giving human being."

She hiccups. Still sexy.

"He'd get along great with *my* ex," I grumble. Phoebe appears before my eyes again, in a haze of alcoholic wistfulness. I can almost feel her small waist in my hands again, her long, creamy leg hiking up around me. I haven't missed her in a while—no, I haven't *allowed* myself to miss her—but just now she comes roaring back into my brain. I can see her beautiful face again, full of judgment. Full of disappointment. "Nothing was ever good enough for her. No, nothing *I* did was good enough."

"Why do women not notice a good thing when it's right in front of them?" Julia says. She kisses me back, and my erection is reaching urgent status. I break off gently.

"She does now. She's got her soul mate." I put the word into air quotes. "They're so in love. Met at a fucking Cubs game. The Cubs, for fuck's sake! Is that a bad omen or what? They'll never make it to the World Series, you know?"

"I know," Julia says, nodding sagely, like what I said made perfect sense. Which it did. Because I'm awesome.

"He works in the sales department of an air conditioner manufacturing company something or other." Who can focus on details at a time like this? I put my hand on Julia's knee. God, her skin is so fucking soft. "She left her practice, you know? On track for a partnership in Chicago, top law firm, and she quits to run out to Nevada with some asshole she just met." I raise my shot glass. "Here's to Hank Jessup. Good thing he's an air conditioner man in a desert; he will never run out of work."

I down my drink. Julia gapes at me.

"Are you kidding me? She went all the way out to Vegas just to be with some guy she met at a baseball game?" Julia strikes her chest. "I write romance, and even *I* think that's a pretty fucking stupid thing to do."

"'Cause you're smart." I lean in, my vision wavering slightly, enjoying the sight of her splitting into two Julias. Two Julias are better than one. Tyler swore he'd get me a threesome while I was here; I won the jackpot, buddy. "You're so fucking smart."

"No, *you're* so smarting fuck," she whispers, then kisses me. This is a debate for the ages. Being drunk with a stranger is the best present I could've given myself. Thank you, Mike and Stacy. I hope you have lots of scorching hot honeymoon sex.

"If I could find your ex, I'd kick his ass all the way downtown," I mutter against her lips. Not even sure that makes sense, but screw it. Screw everything.

Julia pulls away a little, a wry little smile quirking up her lips. "The feeling's mutual," she purrs, trailing her fingers along my jaw.

"I hate men who turn into mewling bitches because their wives make money," I say, feeling my annoyance at whatever jackass she was married to rising. "Don't give me shit about your fucking fragile masculinity. Get a better job, asshole. No one's stopping you."

I'm serious about that, too. I've seen men come into my office whining about how their wives are parasites who stay home all day and drain them of their hard-earned money. Then, a second later, other guys show up bitching about how their wives are emasculating them by working for a living. I mean, make up your mind, dickwads.

"Thank you," Julia moans, tilting her head back and exposing her beautiful throat. "God, it's so nice to hear that all men aren't cavemen."

"Unless we want to be," I murmur, kissing down her neck and sliding my hand into her dress. I slip under her bra, feeling her nipple peaking and getting hard. "Unless we want to grab a woman by the hair, bend her over a table . . . "

"That sounds good," she murmurs, breathless. She moans as I squeeze her nipple, her luscious lips parting with need.

"That's it," the cowboy bartender says, slamming our bill onto the bar. "Out." He folds his arms over his gingham-plaid shirt, and spits a stream of tobacco juice into a bucket under the bar.

This is a classy establishment, as you can see.

We pay and wander back onto the street, Julia hanging onto my shoulder. The Vegas air is a warm embrace even in the middle of the night. The sky above is soft, black velvet, the world around us awash and hazy with city lights. Julia kisses me again, wrapping herself around me. Damn, I want to get her back to the hotel and into my bed. I kiss her, harder and more demanding, but she pulls back.

"Wait. You said your ex is in Vegas? You ever get tempted to call her while you're here?" she asks, running a hand through my hair.

"Why? Jealous?" I ask, grinning as I lean in for a kiss. But she denies me again.

"Don't you wanna, like, give her a piece of your mind?"

"Nah," I say, shrugging. Like it's easy. Though it feels easy right now, with Julia in my arms. "She's got her air conditioner and her fucking parrot. She loved that thing. Peebles was the one nice thing about her moving out; no more parrot shit on everything in the living room."

"Hold on," Julia says, putting a hand on my chest. Her smile stretches out, impossibly wide. "What would you say to a little home invasion?"

I blink, not understanding. But when she explains her plan in depth, I can't stop grinning either.

Is this legal? Abso-fucking-lutely not. But tequila, man. Tequila's a helluva drug.

———

"WE ARE the world's greatest parrot-nappers," Julia hisses at me as we climb out of the Uber. The driver looks over his shoulder at me, a querying expression on his face.

"This is being done for the good of the nation," I tell him, giving him my best lawyer face. I can feel it; the muscles in my cheeks go slack every time. The guy only nods and lets me out.

As the car drives away, we do our best to walk in a straight line to the door. I only veer into a bush once, which means I am fucking golden, and I am going to break into a fucking house tonight.

Phoebe and her soul mate live in a subdivision out in the seemingly endless suburbs around the Las Vegas strip.

Similar looking houses, probably beige and cream in the daylight, stand watch all along the street. The streetlights buzz like, like, uh, like buzzing things. Yeah. Buzzing things that watch people.

Watch this, you suburban pricks.

"What if they're home?" I stage whisper to Julia as I follow behind her. My eyes trail to her perfect ass. Maybe we can get back at Phoebe by fucking right here, in the driveway.

She swats my hand away when I go after her. A woman who's all about business; I can get behind that.

"We'll pretend to be Jehovah's Witnesses who forgot their pamphlets. I've done it before in high school," she says, peering in through the window. "It's how I got a look inside rich people's houses. They had chandeliers and no shag carpeting!" She sounds awed by the memory. "Wonder how we can figure out if they're here." She puts her hands on her hips. Very nice hips.

I come up behind her, placing my hands on her waist. I sweep her hair aside and kiss her neck. She gasps a little.

"I think they're gone," I whisper in her ear, and nod at the drive. "This is a one-car garage. Phoebe's Beamer always sits out here; I know because she bitched about it in one of our last breakup emails. If it's gone, so are they. Probably having a night on the town." I try to keep the mockery out of my voice. I don't succeed.

Julia spins around, throws her arms about my neck, and kisses me. I want to keep going—maybe have a quick good luck fuck before breaking in. Like you do. But she pulls away. Dammit.

"Hold on," Julia says, taking off her shoes and throwing them onto the lawn. "Give me a boost."

"For what?" I ask, though I cup my hands and let her step onto them.

There's an overhang above the porch, and Julia climbs up on top of it with my help. She crawls over to the window overlooking the street. The roof above is slanted, and I'm afraid one of the shingles is going to slip and she'll go tumbling off and onto the ground. That fear creates a surge of adrenaline or testosterone or some chemical that reminds me how out of control this could be.

"Are you crazy?" I whisper, blinking rapidly.

Yes, she is crazy. And so am I. Some sane part of me is coming back and yelling in my ear, telling me that, as my lawyer, he advises me to get the fuck out of here. But Julia jimmies the window, and it slides open. She pumps a victorious fist into the air.

"Vegas, baby!" she yells, and then tumbles into the blackness of the open window.

Well, fuck. Better go after the fair drunken damsel. I pull myself up onto the overhang—dead lifting in the gym is useful after all—and slide in after Julia.

I blink, trying to focus my eyes in the darkness. Neither of us is quite drunk or stupid enough to start turning on lights. But I hear her rummaging around some-where down the hall. I landed in the master bedroom, which still has boxes left to be unpacked.

Six damn months later, and Phoebe's still putting shit away. There was a time, when we first moved in together, that she had to have us scrub every corner of the condo before we could even think of putting our boxes in. And then everything was unpacked within twenty-four hours. Living with air conditioner man has made her sloppy.

Or happy. Maybe it's just because she's happy and doesn't need everything on the outside to be perfect, to make up for what isn't there inside.

It's like a bullet to the chest, and I crouch on the floor just to breathe the pain out. The tequila's ripped all my internal walls away, allowing my thoughts to be heard, no matter what they are. I tell myself that my tight-ass, angry phase started after she left, but I know that's not exactly the truth. I could always be a little domineering. A little judgmental. A little arrogant. After all, when I first met Julia I dismissed her based on her fucking suitcase. What kind of asshole does that? I could've missed a connection with a warm, sexy, gorgeous woman simply because she liked shiny purple things.

Maybe I've been using Phoebe's leaving to ignore the things I never liked about myself.

And then I hear Julia knocking around somewhere in this house, and my mood lightens a bit. Fuck this self-reflective moment. I'm having an adventure right now. An adventure in stupid shit. It's not the time for soul searching.

"Where are you?" I say, getting up and stumbling to the door.

"In here!" Julia calls. I follow down the hall, careful not to bang into anything. The darkness tilts and whirls in front of me, like a tilty whirly thing, and it's a little hard to remember what's up and what's down.

In front of me, Julia exits the bathroom, two rolls of toilet paper in hand and a mischievous grin on her face. At least, I think her expression is mischievous. It's still pretty fucking dark in here.

"What are you doing?" I ask, catching one of the rolls as she chucks it to me.

"We're going to do a little redecorating," she giggles, and walks past. She throws her toilet paper up over some light fixtures in the hallway, decorating the lights with reams of fluffy white. Then she breaks it off and ties some paper around the bedroom doorknob.

I smile. Fuck it; it's time to be stupid.

"Watch," I grunt, and toss my roll into a sweeping arc through the air. It spins gracefully, pillowy sheets of paper trailing behind it like streamers. The roll bounces down the staircase, leaving a graceful trail behind. I stumble down the stairs and grab the roll again, heading into the kitchen for more extensive design.

Above me, Julia cackles.

In the kitchen, I hear the familiar squawk of a familiar pain-in-the-ass parrot. "Hey Peebles. Glad to hear you're alive and kicking, you little bastard," I whisper, draping lines of toilet paper over the rustic looking chandelier they've hung in the ceiling.

The bird continues to squawk and move in its cage. I head over and open the door, reaching inside. I can see a dark shape rustling around, and wince as something pecks me. Fucking animal.

"Here, Peebles. Here, you little feathery asshole," I mutter, and I grab the bird. Peebles shrieks and whistles, but I pull him out, grinning down at him in the light from the streetlamps outside. Julia stumbles into the kitchen after me.

"Okay. I'm outta TP. I think we should hit the road." She looks down at her feet. "Where are my shoes?"

"Outside," I say, grabbing her up around the waist and kissing her. I've never felt so alive, with a beautiful woman in my arm and a parrot in my hand. Peebles reminds me of his shitty existence with another peck. "Let's get the hell out of here."

16

JULIA

2:31 AM

"REMEMBER, I've always kept my jacket buttoned like this," I whisper to Nate as we walk into the hotel lobby.

The night guy at the reception desk gives us a surprised look. Well, I *am* barefoot with Nate's jacket draped over my shoulders, plus hugging myself like I have a terrible stomach problem. Well, I got ninety-nine problems right now, and a bird smuggled in under my hookup's jacket is the most pressing one.

Put *that* into the song, musical person.

"You look like you have a hernia," he whispers back.

But for you, baby, it'll be a sexy hernia.

"Look, we're getting stares. Where do we go now?" I hiss. Nate keeps his hand on my back—and guides it a little lower to my ass. Instantly, heat floods my core, moving lower.

Fuck it. I'm into it. Let's have sex on top of the parrot.

Fortunately, he's a little more focused on business right now than I am.

"Follow me," he says, and guides me past the front

desk and the elevator bank, and out onto the casino floor. Even at whatever o'clock this is, there are still people on the slots and at the tables. Time works differently in a Vegas casino, same as in an Indian opium den, or watching that fourth *Transformers* movie. You're never quite sure when you started, and you have a vague idea of when you'll finish. For all you know, you've been here for years.

"Over here," Nate says, hooking an arm around me and taking me through to a long, echoing corridor.

Ah, I know where we're going. The hotel has a conservatory.

We emerge into a jungle-like glen, with palm trees and fake rock walls, and high above us, a domed glass ceiling to let in the sunlight. It's Japanese cherry blossom season, and there's a kind of teahouse overlooking a small, fake pond. Paper birds, made from bright pink and yellow paper, soar above us on strings. The air smells of magnolia and cherry blossom; bright bursts of hibiscus flare around us.

And boom: there are the birds.

There are cages of parrots, and some birds flying free around the room. I look up, agog. "I didn't know this hotel had birds."

That is my brilliant contribution to this conversation. Envy me, for I am a wordsmith.

"Maybe Peebles would like it here," he says, as I unbutton my coat and pull out the squawking bird.

Damn. His wings are strong as shit. He flaps them, whacking me in the face a couple of times. *Fuck you, bird.*

"I hate the name Peebles. Maybe change it to Francois.

Or Millicent. Whatever, here you go, birdy!" I whisper, and toss him up into the air.

The parrot flaps his wings and soars up to whistle and click with all the other birds. Well, if I was a parrot, I'd rather live in a dense indoor tropical jungleland than a cage in someone's Vegas subdivision. *Good luck, Peebles. You nasty little jerk.*

"I think we should go back to my room," Nate whispers in my ear.

My skin thrills a little at his touch, and he traces his hand down my arm. His breath is warm, the scent of alcohol and bad decisions potent like a delicious cologne. I can feel his muscled body pressed up against the line of my back, and it's driving me wild. I have to see him naked.

"I think room we should back to, yes, go," I respond, breathless. Hey, you try making sense while being incredibly horny at the same time.

We head back to the elevators and speed up to the top floor. With Nate's arm in mine, holding me steady, I make it down the lushly carpeted hall and to his door. He fumbles with the key a minute, opens up, and flicks on the lights.

I enter the foyer and whistle, taking it all in. Damn.

"Who did you have to screw to get a penthouse?" I murmur, leaning against him as he kicks the door closed with his foot. Ahead of us, floor to ceiling windows offer a view of the Vegas Strip, lights shimmering, bursts of neon exploding in the distance.

"My client's ex-wife," he says. When my eyebrows shoot up, Nate chuckles. "My firm represents people with a lot to lose in divorce settlements. A particular owner of a huge amount of Vegas property was going through a rather messy divorce. Supermodel married him, cheated on him, and still thought she was entitled to half." He shrugs. "He didn't see it coming, poor idiot."

"Well, I'm sure he married her for their compatibility and mutual love and respect," I say, rolling my eyes. "I don't get why some people think marriage is about collecting trophies."

"I don't disagree," he says, while we walk into the living room. He kisses the back of my neck. "But he was pretty desperate. And I managed to buy her off with a fraction of what she was after."

"No wonder you don't think much of romance," I sigh. He flips on a light in the living room. I do something of a double take. "Then again, with hotel rooms like these, I don't think it bothers you much."

The room is sunken, two carpeted steps down and you're in a vast living area replete with soft white couches. The coffee table is polished black wood, the drapes by the windows deep violet silk.

"I get to stay for free," Nate says, sliding an arm around my waist, cradling me against his body. He sounds a little proud. And hell, he probably should be. "The perks of being a corrupt, heartless lawyer."

"Hey now." I turn and shake a finger at him. "I never said you were corrupt."

He laughs, that rich, melodious sound that slides down my skin and liquefies my panties. Nate presses me against his body. His mouth finds mine, the kiss scorching hot. The slight stubble on his face rasps against my cheek. I sigh, melting into his arms.

"You think we should get cleaned up?" he whispers in my ear.

Mmm, a nice hot shower. Just what I need.

Plus, I was bird-handling for a while. I should wash my hands.

"Lead the way." I grin at him as we head into the bathroom, which is pretty much a marble palace all on its own. I blink in the soft mood lighting from the sconces on the wall. No fluorescents in this baby. Man, maybe going into divorce law is the way to enjoy the good things.

That's a depressing thought.

Then Nate slides his hand under my shirt, and anything depressing gets shot out of a cannon and sent far, far away.

"Now, now. Why don't you run the water?" I say, turning around and ghosting my lips against his mouth.

He growls low in his throat, an animal sound. I love it. He turns on the shower, and I admire the view as he pulls his shirt up over his head. Fucking in that closet was fun, but I didn't get to enjoy the sensational sights now on display. His chest is rock-hard and muscled, with a distinct six-pack of abs that I'd like to explore. A line of dark hair leads into his boxers, and when he pulls those down . . . well. His ass is spectacularly sculpted.

Lucky me.

Heh. Getting lucky. Luck. Vegas. If I wasn't so tipsy, there'd be so many ways to spin that joke.

"Aren't you afraid we'll be interrupted?" I ask as I unclasp my bra. Then I unzip my skirt, and get into the shower.

Nate grins and follows me, a wicked light in his eyes.

Wicked is my favorite kind of light. And my favorite musical.

Okay. No show tunes right now, Julia. There's a time and a place for all things.

"Mike's rarely in his room here. He wanted to be with Stacy. I think Tyler's still out on the Strip somewhere. Probably horndogging it around town," he says, kissing my bare shoulder. I groan as he joins me under the hot water, the glass stall steaming up around us.

"I'm sorry I pulled you away from your bachelor party," I say, hitching my leg up around his waist. Already, I can feel his cock hardening, pushing against me. We kiss again, and Nate nibbles at my jaw, my neck.

"I think Mike and Stacy are having a better time just by themselves." He grins down at me, and we kiss. I get lost in it, and he tightens his arms around my body. "They don't have nearly as much fun apart as they do together."

"That's the kind of love everyone looks out for," I say, my mouth wandering down his neck. I also circle my hand around his fully-erect cock. My fingers trail along its length, and I earn a hiss that melts into a moan.

"Maybe. But in a pinch, sex with a beautiful woman in a shower will do," he growls against my mouth.

I grin, peppering kisses up his jawline, then down the other side of his neck. I go lower, lower until I'm on my knees in front of him, eye level with his shaft.

I wink up at him, and he gasps. "What are you doing?"

"One guess," I say, and lick him. One of those nice, slow licks, introducing the head of his cock to my tongue and earning a sharp inhale. I pull back just enough to press a delicate kiss across his crown before I take him into my mouth, easing him in slowly.

Nate groans, and I grip his thighs, rock-hard and perfectly muscled. And I can't help it—I groan, myself, the sound guttural and deep. I take him deep with a hard suck. My hand closes around the base of his cock, offering a consolatory squeeze, and my head begins to rock back and forth.

"Jesus, your mouth is fucking perfect," he whispers, bracing one hand against the shower stall. "Keep going."

I taste him very slowly, exploring his every thick, throbbing inch. He tastes wonderful, salt and steel. My tongue swirls and explores, lapping around him, caressing his cockhead every time I pull away. I'm not sure what he likes more, so I give it all to him. A long suck and then a lick of my tongue. A hard pull and a squeeze of my hand. Nate's groans grow louder and more frequent, his body lined with tension, and I'm kinda addicted to him being at my mercy.

"Julia," he whispers, his voice throaty.

"Mmm," I respond. I squeeze the base of his shaft again, then suck him all the way, deeper than before, as deep as I can go. I feel him brush the back of my throat and instinctively swallow, reveling in his hitching breath, the slight tremble in his legs. It's not a position I can hold long, but I take my time when I draw him out again, my lips pulling on every inch of his delicious skin. When only the tip of him remains in my mouth, I compress my lips around it, and give it a good, long lick.

That's when Nate tries to move, to take control of the situation. I put one hand to his hip, and he stills. He's mine to play with and torment right now. And, judging by the ragged sound of his breathing, he couldn't be happier about it.

I move faster, my other hand taking its place again at the base of his cock, pumping and squeezing up and down in tandem with pulls of my mouth. For a moment, it's that—my head bobbing, his taste everywhere, his skin feverish under my fingers, his legs beginning to tremble as I take his cock again and again and again. Then I change my pace, slowing, languid, giving my tongue time to swirl and savor. Every time I edge back, I pay special attention to his cockhead, not too much pressure—just enough to have him *really* moan.

"Fuck yes," he gasps.

Then I switch again, sucking harder, faster, and stroking what part of him I can't take into my mouth at this pace.

Nate groans again, his voice getting raspier. "I can't hold on much longer." He grips my hair, his hips thrusting, his cock pistoning in and out of my mouth. I let him this time, savoring his urgency, the raw need in his voice, the way his balls nearly brush my chin every time he drives himself in. He's tense all over, and I know it's about to burst.

His breaths cadence the air, his body's tremors intensifying. I know he wants deeper, wants the back of my throat again, and I want that, too. But his need sends white hot sparks through my body, and I realize for the first time how wet I am. That part of the ache I feel is due to the pulsing between my legs. I slip a hand down my stomach and cup my heated pussy, my fingers rolling over my clit as my mouth strides to keep up with the thrusts of his cock. I jolt, and it feels so good I caress myself again.

When Nate sees what I am doing, the animal look in his magnetic eyes grows even wilder. "You have no idea what you're doing to me," he rasps.

Oh, I think I do.

I slide my tongue along his length again, dragging my fingers down my wet slit as I do, until the head of his cock is again at my throat, and I work my muscles around him. He trembles and murmurs—or cries—my name, so I do it again. And again, and again, and *fucking yes* again. I can taste how close he is, feel how badly he needs it, and damn, I need it, too. I can't remember the last time I wanted to give myself over to a man like this, feel him swell on my tongue, hear him call my name in a desperate voice as I drive him onward to the edge, leave him hanging, then onward and onward until . . . .

"Fuck," Nate groans, throwing his head back. I take him in a final time until he reaches the back of my throat, and I swallow and I swallow and I swallow, and he explodes, fast and hot, spilling himself in a nosedive of control.

A moment later I pull back, releasing him, and wipe off the sides of my mouth. Like a lady, dammit. I stand and smile at him.

Nate is pressed back against the marble wall, his eyes half lidded.

"I think I did all right," I muse, appreciating the sight of my handiwork.

"Better than all right," he murmurs, and pulls me to him, kissing me hungrily. His hands trail over my breasts, my nipples peaking beneath his attention. "I think you deserve a reward," he breathes before kissing me again.

He palms my breasts just long enough to thumb my nipples before snaking an arm around me, holding me against him. He slides his other hand between my legs, which are now trembling, and picks up where I left off, strumming my clit, gently at first but gaining urgency. I gasp and buck in his arms.

"Easy, baby. I want to listen to you come," he whispers in my ear, rubbing the wet seam of my pussy before poising a finger at my opening. He nips my lower lip, presses down on my clit with his thumb, then slowly eases his finger into me.

I keen and groan. Nate watches me, his eyes alight with desire. He gasps as I groan, biting my bottom lip as his attentions spark a feeling in me.

God, how can I already be on the edge? This man's a magician.

Hard to believe that a few hours ago I thought he was cold. He's passionate, domineering, everything I'd want in a hero in one of my books. But he's with me tonight, here and in the flesh. After Drew, I thought I'd never experience anything like it again. Hell, I thought I'd never experience it, period. This kind of lust, all-consuming, furious, passionate, I've never had anything like it.

I kiss him, taste him, grow bolder.

"Oh, fuck. Fuck me with your mouth," I whisper. The thrusts of his hand slow, then stop altogether. His thumb remains poised over my clit, just close enough for me to feel it.

He smiles. "Perfect," he whispers.

Some mad genius decided to install this shower with a

ledge, probably so Nate could ease me onto it and perch
so readily between my wide, eager legs. He dips his head
and runs that magic tongue around my nipple before
swallowing my breast. He sucks hard enough to earn a
whimper before pulling back again. Then he drags his
mouth across my chest until his lips are at my other
breast, his tongue licking away rivulets of water. He
makes sure I know just how much he loves my breasts
before slowly kissing his way down my body, alternating
with licks and sucks here and there, trailing down my
belly until . . . .

Yes. Right there, please.

Nate rubs my legs, his hands sweeping along my inner
thigh and toward my aching cunt, but not touching me
where I need him most. He leans down and exchanges his
hands for his mouth, traces a line of kisses up my sensitive flesh, his stubble a teasing whisper. The sensation is
glorious, electric, and enticing.

Then I feel his hot breath on my sex, and his tongue
makes a playful lap of my clit. I gasp, but he holds me in
place, still exploring, still teasing. He licks me again and
drags his tongue in languid circles around my clit before
drawing a line to the mouth of my pussy and pushing
inside.

Oh fucking God, yes.

He strokes once, twice, then his fingers replace his
tongue, which returns obediently to my clit, and I
whimper louder. I feel myself tighten around his fingers,
every inch of skin he touches seemingly on fire—a miracle
since I'm sopping wet—and it's so good I can't look away.
He plunges into me over and over, traces me with his
tongue, sucks me with his mouth. I writhe, wiggling my

hips, thrusting my pussy against his face, and he answers my call by wrapping his lips around my clit and giving a good tug. I throw my head back, my body whining when he pulls his fingers out of me, then screaming in joy when his tongue takes over, teasing flesh so sensitive it feels electric. I could ride his tongue for hours, but then his fingers are back, pushing, thrusting, and I could ride those, too. Especially when his mouth returns to my clit, circling and sucking.

I am right on the edge, seams full to bursting. Nate pauses for a moment, which makes me want to scream, but he looks up into my eyes. His gaze is magnificent, possessing me.

"You're so beautiful," he whispers, then his tongue is back on me, flattened, his fingers pushing inside me.

I'm shaking so hard I'm going to rupture, the sounds coming out of my mouth wild. I slap the wall to ground myself.

"Nate. Make me come. Please." I groan.

He closes his lips around my clit and pulls again. And again. And again. His thrusting fingers slip in and out of me, and my stomach tightens as every muscle in my legs goes rigid. I'm cresting, riding the wave. I start to pant, the steam rising all around me, Nate's tongue insistent and probing, driving me wild.

I cry out, screaming his name as I come, the world around me flashing and breaking apart like a shattered mirror. I go limp and slump forward. Nate stands and catches me, holding me against his chest. He kisses me, and I can taste myself on his lips, along with tequila and a little victory.

"Did that live up to your expectations?" he whispers.

It did. Looking up at him, the wild and aggressive light in his eyes is still intoxicating. He looks at me with need, with desire. I haven't been wanted like that in a long time.

Come to think of it, I don't think Drew ever gazed at me like that; like watching me come and scream his name was all he wanted, all he'd ever want.

I can't remember feeling this happy.

"Exceeded my expectations, actually." I grin as we kiss. "I think we should get out. I'm starting to prune." I hold up my hands for his inspection, and he laughs.

"Still beautiful," he says, kissing my palm. The water's begun to cool a little bit, but I don't really notice.

17

NATE

WE'RE LYING in bed now, the sheets tangled around us. Julia's leg is over mine. The sensation of her skin is almost overwhelming. It's soft, beautiful; hell, it's perfect. What is it about this woman, where the barest contact gets me hard? Even though I got one of the best blowjobs of my life in the shower, I can feel myself ready to go again.

But first, sustenance. I sit up, passing a hand over my head to smooth my hair. It doesn't take. I don't really care.

"Ready for more champagne?" I ask Julia. The room service cart is still at the foot of the bed, an iced bottle of Veuve Clicquot waiting to pour another glass, a bowl of ripe strawberries beside it. Technically room service is closed, but it's never out of service for the VIPs. Life's good at the top of the world. Or the top of a Vegas hotel.

Either way, being me is fucking sweet right about now.

"You never say no to champagne. Especially when studly naked men are pouring. Mom always told me that," Julia says, handing over her empty glass.

I get out of bed and pour, watching her appreciate my

form. She looks damn good herself. Her tits are still on display, round and perfectly proportioned.

Why is it whenever I look at this woman, I feel myself losing control? I never liked that before. I never liked feeling that way with Phoebe. There's something about Julia that gets me horny and makes me relax all at once.

I think this is what bliss feels like. I hand the fizzing glass back to her.

"She added the part about studly, naked men?" I ask.

Julia sips and luxuriates. She tilts her head back, a smile on her face, her eyes closed. I like a woman who appreciates things.

"Maybe those weren't Mom's precise words. Hey, I'm a writer. I take creative license," she purrs, sitting up. The sight of her, naked and twined in the sheets, her hair cascading all around her flushed face . . . yep, there I go. My favorite body part has raised its flag, ready for another conquest. I haven't felt like this since I was nineteen years old. We're barely dry from the shower yet.

Julia grins, appreciating the view. "Good morning to you, too," she says, flopping back onto the bed. I take that as an invitation and kiss her, tasting the champagne and strawberries on her lips. I trail kisses down her chest, her breasts, slipping back the sheets to reveal—

"Hold on, hold on. Don't you believe in savoring things?" she asks, rolling away from me. Tease. But she laughs. From her, I don't mind the laughing.

Was there ever a time when I thought the sound of it was annoying? I was an idiot.

"Lawyer, remember?" I point to myself. "I like to cut through the endless discussion and take charge." I lie back next to her.

Julia puts her champagne glass on the bedside table and looks at me. There's curiosity in her gaze. That and a little lust, which I'm happy to see.

"So no foreplay, Mr. Wexler? Or is it counselor Wexler? Barrister Wexler? Wexler the lawyer?" She props her chin up on her hand.

"I never said no foreplay. Far from it. I just don't like endless talking." I kiss her shoulder, her back . . . and she rolls away again.

Somehow, the teasing is turning me on even more.

"Well, again, writer here." She points to herself. "My characters always start off with a little talk."

I snort. Can't help it. "Guys don't really want that. The whole verbal thing before sex. That is pure female fantasy right there."

She juts her chin in defiance. "You haven't heard my characters yet."

"All right." I lie back and give her a challenging look. "Show me."

"Huh?" She looks surprised. Gotcha.

"Grab one of your books and show me. You must have something written on your laptop." I spy the case at the foot of the bed.

When the hell did we get that? Must've gone down to her room at some point. Shit, it's not good that I'm having blackout moments.

Julia untangles herself from the sheets and pulls up her computer. For the first time, she looks at me shyly, almost like she's embarrassed.

"Okay, I haven't read this scene aloud yet. You're the first to hear it."

"You read your books aloud?" I don't mean that to

sound mocking, but she stiffens. *Idiot.* "I only meant that I didn't know you spent that much time on them."

"Wow. Condescension, thy name is Wexler," she says dryly, booting up her laptop.

Shut the fuck up, Nate. You have a beautiful naked woman with a computer in your bed, and all you can do is give her shit?

"Asshole comes with the lawyer job. Sort of an accessory, like a Rolex watch or eating lunch at your desk." I hold my hands up. "I'm trying to get rid of it."

I think she accepts it, because she turns back to her screen.

"All right. So this is right before Archer and Lola have sex for the first time. I mean, like, not going down on each other. This is the full consummation." She brushes hair out of her eyes and holds up her hands; she's setting the scene. "Archer's a billionaire with a dark secret, and Lola is trying to weasel it out of him. Industrial espionage, you know. But she's falling in love with him, wants him to dominate her utterly, and he's arousing in her all of these feelings she never knew she had, and he knows it. And he wants her to give in." She peeks over at me. "Don't laugh."

"Scout's honor," I say, sitting up and propping myself against the pillowed headrest.

She clears her throat and starts reading. " 'You're a woman of secrets and shadows, Lola. You were born in the darkness, but that's not where you belong. Don't fight it. Don't fight me.' Archer passed his hand up Lola's thigh, fingers toying at the lace edge of her panties. She stifled a moan, but a shudder ran through her body, betraying her.

" 'A spy doesn't do well in the sunlight,' she replied, licking *her lips partly out of nervousness, partly because she knew it would turn him on. The sharp intake of his breath told her she'd judged him correctly. His eyes darkened with need. Yet his fingers continued their exploration. She quivered, wanting to feel the thick length of him pushing inside her, thrusting, possessing her as she finally surrendered herself, body and soul. Archer pressed a kiss against her neck, gentle and yet amazingly cruel.*

" *'I want you to give yourself to me,' he murmured, his breath hot against her throat. 'I want to feel you beneath me, gasping as I slide myself into you. I want to feel you shudder as my cock fills you, stretches you. I want you to cry out as I move inside you, urging me on. Giving yourself to me fully, your body begging for me as I take you. I want to make you come. And I want it now.' His hands moving freely down her back now. 'Don't you understand, Lola, that I always get what I want?' He unzipped her Chanel dress deftly, and it pooled at her feet, a whisper of surrender.' "*

As she reads, Julia's gaze softens. She's lying on her stomach, chin cupped in her hand, the naked expanse of her back open to me. I'm looking at her now, fully appreciating her. The slight sunburn at her shoulder, the thin white tan line of her bra strap standing out in sharp contrast. The freckles that dust her back. The way she curls her hair idly around her finger as she reads. Her right foot bobbing up and down, keeping time with the lilt and lull of her voice. All of it, suddenly, seems beautiful to me. As I lie there, watching her, I realize that the waiting is beginning to kill me. I want her underneath me, but her voice, her words, are conjuring images in my mind. And I like it.

" *'Do you always get what you want?' she asked him*

breathlessly as his mouth met hers again. His fingers ghosted across the lace of her bra. He unclasped it, and it fell at his feet. The night air was a cold kiss against her breasts, and he took them in his hands. Drawing her closer, he allowed her to unbutton his dress shirt, which was still impeccably starched from the opera. Her hands traveled over his rock-hard abs, appreciating the contours. He claimed her lips, tasting her, taking everything from her, giving everything to her. She unbuttoned his pants, gasping with need, and reached down to seize him, urgent and throbbing in her hand. He—"

"Stop," I say. My voice is harsh, almost guttural. Julia looks up in wide-eyed surprise. I get on my knees, lean over, and flip the laptop lid closed. She gazes up at me, a playful, knowing light in her eyes.

"What's the rush?" she whispers. I lean down and kiss her. When she tries to get up, I grip her around the waist.

"Right there," I whisper, then lean over and bite her shoulder softly. Julia moans, and I reach over for the strip of condoms still laid out on the bedside table.

God bless bachelorette parties.

An instant later, my cock sheathed, I lower myself onto her, still holding her in place. I tease myself along her pussy, and she squirms, wiggling against me.

I slide a hand to cup her cunt, slipping between her sodden flesh, and spear a finger inside her. Thank fuck, she's ready. I wonder idly if reading her own material turns her on, or if that happy job is mine alone, but then I find it doesn't matter. I position my cock where I want it most and then—oh yes—I'm sliding inside her. Like before, she grips me, and it'd be so easy to sink to the hilt, but I want to tease her. I begin pumping, my pace unhurried, every nerve in my body on fucking overload.

When she gasps, I slip a hand between us again and finger her clit.

"Oh, fuck me," she groans, putting her forehead onto the bed. "Don't stop."

"I will," I say, "and I won't." Then I thrust my cock all the way in, root-deep. Her cunt grips me, squeezing and tight and oh so perfect. She moans, and something primal ripples through me.

Those sounds are mine. I pause, painful as it is, and breathe. Otherwise I'll come right now, and I'm not ready for this to be over. I want to enjoy it. "You want it like this," I growl as I begin moving, dragging my cock in and out of her, mesmerized by her silky, wet skin, the way she squeezes and pulls at me. "You want me to take you all the way."

"Yes," Julia gasps. She glances at me over her shoulder, and rolls her hips. Again. Again. She gives as good as she gets.

I fuck her hard, ride her, my thrusts accented by her staccato breaths. I tap her clit again before scaling my hands to cup her breasts, rubbing my palms against the perfect peaks of her nipples. Julia lifts her hips, and I slam into her, my muscles tightening, straining, but I'm so hungry for her it doesn't matter. She meets me each time I pound inside, her pussy squeezing, burning me, and it feels so good it could make a grown man cry. My body is fueled with the need to feel her like this always, riding my cock, desperate for it, squeezing me to oblivion as I enter her again and again and again.

I want her to know I've been here, that she's mine.

Each time I thrust inside, it's to the hilt, so as much of me as possible is in her—she feels all of it, and I feel all of her. And fuck me, she loves it. Her face is flushed, her lips parted, her eyes closed. I drag my fingers around her nipples, pinch them. Then I slide one hand down her stomach, to the slick spot between her thighs, and find her clit again.

She starts keening. "Yes!" Her voice takes on a new, desperate pitch. "There, fuck, don't stop!"

She grinds against me, licking her lips. Fuck. I've never wanted to come so hard in my life; I've also never wanted anything to last more than this, because every second is so goddamn good. She's so tight, and she gets tighter, wetter, every time my cock hits home. She's so fucking close now. So am I. I want to explode, detonate while I'm buried deep inside of her.

I fist her hair and pull her face to mine. Julia kisses me, her tongue searching my mouth, stroking my tongue as I massage her clit faster, pump inside her harder. She's gasping. Fuck it, I'm about to come . . . .

"Not yet," she whispers, her hips stilling.

I understand. Somehow, it comes through the haze. And I pull out. It's torture, but I do it. I'm sitting up, and she gets to her knees, turns and straddles me. Then her perfect cunt, wet and pink and *mine*, lines up with my cock again, and I'm back inside of her. All the way in. A low growl throbs in my throat as her hips begin undulating. She works me in and out of her, her eyes cloudy, her lips parted. Her tits bounce with each spear of my cock inside her. Her eyes lock onto mine, and her pupils dilate as she begins riding me in earnest. I can tell she's close, and fuck, so am I. Watching her face, her swaying breasts, the sweat lacing her skin—watching my cock, slick with her juices, disappear into her pussy again and again is enough to drive any man mad. I grip her by the waist and guide her, pumping up into her, meeting her motions perfectly.

We ride each other.

"God, you're so fucking big," she whispers against my lips, teasing me with a kiss.

"How is your pussy so tight?" I whisper, then take her breast into my mouth, feeling her nipple harden on my tongue.

God, I'm going to come so fast.

"A year without sex'll do that." She moans, and throws her head back.

I kiss up her neck.

"My ex was the last man I was with, before you," she says.

"Your ex is a fucking moron," I grunt. The scent of her skin, her sweat, the way her pussy clamps around my cock, it's overwhelming. I can feel it, the tension, the orgasm building.

"Fuck the memory out of me," she whispers, swallowing me in another kiss.

Let no one say I don't accept challenges. I push her back onto the bed, falling on top of her, and thrust as hard and fast as my hips will allow. It's a pounding rhythm, and when she begins to whisper my name, I know she's on the verge of climax, and something inside me goes off. I jerk, coming hard inside her, the world around me shaking and collapsing, crying out as she comes right along with me. Her wail is high and perfect, her head tilted back, her body bucking against mine.

After a moment, I slow, and finally stop. I'm laying on top of her, breathing as hard as I can, her breasts pushed up against me. Julia sighs as I slide out of her, and soon my chest is at her back. My hand trails over her breasts, enjoying the sensation.

"Was that as good as your books?" I whisper in her ear. She nearly purrs in response.

"Not as choreographed, maybe. And I'm definitely not working for secret shadow organizations of the United States government. But aside from that? Just about as good."

I can't stop touching her, loving the silky feeling of her skin. I've never been this easily aroused by a woman before, not even with Phoebe. I've never had a hunger that I couldn't satisfy. I expect that to piss me off, or scare me, and am surprised when it doesn't. I like everything about this. Considering where this day started for us, who'd have ever thought this would happen?

"You want to know something dumb?" she says. I kiss her shoulder.

"I don't think you could say anything dumb. Unless you ask me what clouds are made of," I say. She playfully smacks my arm.

"I'm afraid I'll wake up and this will all be a dream." She sighs.

"The parrot-napping? Or the sex?" I ask.

"Both got me off, so let's go with both," she deadpans.

We laugh, and I kiss her again. I taste champagne, strawberries, sex, and cherry lip gloss. It's a potent combination.

"We're going to remember this night for a long time," I say, looking deep into her eyes.

18

JULIA

FUCK, I can't believe we forgot about last night. Or at least, we did for a while.

Now I think it's come back to both of us at about the same speed. Which is making this cab ride super fucking awkward. The air between us is so thick with sexual tension you could slice it and put it on sandwiches.

I've got my hand folded in my lap, just to make sure I don't touch him. Nate's focused on staring out the window at the fascinating desert landscape. His throat moves as he swallows; it's like I'm hypnotized by it.

My God, the way he rode me, and the orgasm . . . . How the fuck had I forgotten the orgasm?

"On the bright side," Nate says, carefully not looking at me, "I think I realized where your laptop is."

Once we're back in the hotel, we ride the elevator up to his suite. Open the door, go into the bedroom, and bam. Right there in its cute little cherry red laptop case, set up on the now-made bed. Turndown service must have found it. It's waiting all lonesome for me to scoop it up in my arms and go write more sex scenes.

Hello, beautiful. Mommy missed you.

"How much do you remember now?" Nate asks casually, pacing over to look out the window at the Las Vegas streets below. I stand there, looking over the bed. It's got its pillows all plumped and in place, probably put on new sheets. The evidence of last night is all cleaned up. But the memories are a little tougher to scrub away.

Hey, that was good. Maybe I should put that in a Lola scene, when she's straddling . . . never mind. Not the time or place for work.

"My memories are pretty clear now. We were naked a lot of the time." I'm pretty sure I'm flushing all the way to the edge of my sundress, but that could just be the sunburn. You know, from being in the goddamn desert. "That part was okay. The naked bits. Parts. Whatever." Stop, tongue. Stop it now. "Dammit, where's Christopher Eccleston when I need him?" I moan.

"Who?" Nate asks, looking perplexed.

Awesome. Said it out loud. Go me. I look at him, and I find myself tracing the lines of his shoulder, the way his now sweaty shirt clings to the definitions of his chest and abs. *Damn.* Normally lawyers don't have that much time to hit the gym. Unless he's built this way naturally . . . .

"Your eye is twitching," Nate says with concern, coming over to look at me. "Are you all right?"

Can I just hit rewind on this and go back in time?

"I remember everything," I mumble, gazing down at my feet. "The shower. After the shower. Champagne and strawberries. Maybe that was the final glass that did us in, you know? Tipped us over into memory-wiping boozeville."

"But we did remember," Nate says, moving closer to me.

God, the way his dark blue gaze rakes over my body, it leaves me trembling, my panties growing damper by the second. He brushes his fingertips down the length of my arm, and I shiver in response. I've never had such a reaction before, and especially not to someone who, on most occasions, has been nothing but an asshole. I've always dated nothing but nice, comforting guys.

Then again, Drew was a nice, comforting guy who couldn't handle a successful woman and retreated with his tail between his legs. Where did playing it safe get me? Exactly nowhere.

But I'm not thinking about that any longer. Because Nate's here right now, and there is growing electricity between us. I can feel it, raising the hairs along my arms.

"Do you like remembering?" I ask, looking up at him. I place my hand on his chest, right above his heart. It's beating faster and faster; always a good sign. *What the hell? Live like your fantasies a little, Julia.* I raise myself up lightly on my toes, just brushing my lips against his as I speak. "Did it turn you on?"

"It did," he growls, and kisses me.

It's light and quick at first, the heat between us sizzling as he pulls away. Damn, I don't want him to do that.

I gasp when he pulls me tight against his body, trailing his hand down my back. I like it when he grabs my ass and finds my mouth again, kissing me deeply. Oh God.

My clit's already throbbing as I pull him backwards, falling onto the bed with him on top of me.

He kisses me with his eyes open, watching me. His hand glides slowly up my leg, my skirt falling around my waist. Almost to the magic spot, but he slides his hand back down again. Away from the magic spot.

"How the hell are you doing this to me?" he whispers, looking down at me with a puzzled, horny expression. His gaze is smoldering, confused, wild. "I can't remember the last time I felt this . . . "

He swallows, maybe afraid of the next word.

I don't even think, and I barrel ahead. "Alive," I add. For a second I wince, afraid that the word he was looking for was *moist*.

But he smiles, and kisses me again, his tongue probing my mouth. I moan and arch my back, moving against him. I can feel his erection pressing into me. Damn, I want to fuck him again. Like now. Right now. No passing *Go*. No collecting two hundred dollars.

Nate's hand slips up under my dress, his fingers tracing my bra. My nipples come to attention at once under his touch, and I gasp. He starts to pull at my strap, to take my dress off . . . .

"Wait. Hold on," I say, trying to sit up.

Nate is off me at once, lying back on the bed and staring at the ceiling. His chest rises and falls rapidly with his breathing; looks like he needs to calm down. And judging by the tent he's pitching, maybe take a cold shower as well.

"Sorry. Didn't mean to stop . . . that." I swallow. "I just can't go around having these fun *Love in the Afternoon* type montages until we know for sure whether we are or are not. You know." I pause.

"Married," Nate adds, finishing my sentence.

"I was going to say dehydrated, but yeah. That works too." Nothing like a little humor to lighten the mood. Or lower the erection.

Finally, Nate sighs and sits up. I'm glad we're going to have an actual discussion about this like actual adults, even if David Tennant is stomping his little white tennis shoes all pissed off that he isn't fucking a Chicago lawyer right now.

"What's the next step?" Nate asks, as I get off the bed and adjust myself. You know. Like a lady. "Shit, we need to figure out what we're doing fast. The wedding." He rubs his face, curses softly. "Mike and Stacy's wedding's in a few hours. We have time, right?"

He looks over at me. He's lucky he's in the groom's party. If he were a bridesmaid, he'd be in the hotel room with Stacy for the rest of the afternoon to help get her ready. Guys, they can just show up twenty minutes before the ceremony with their suit in a bag over their shoulder. It's a man's world.

"Yeah, we have time. Obviously, we need to find the chapel. We've got the photos, and there's got to be someone who knows where we went. Maybe we can call that adventure service and ask if I was wearing the veil when we came in last night. That might give us an idea of timeline."

I flip open my phone and stare at the picture. There we are, Nate with lipstick kisses all over his face, Elvis looming over us in the background. Where are you, king of rock 'n roll and shady matrimonial practices?

Just then, the door across the living room opens. Nate's friend with the frosted tips and the affable smile, Tyler, steps in without a shirt on. Nice. Very nice physique. It would be even nicer if we weren't all staring at each other with open mouths and wide eyes.

Tyler looks from me to Nate, and a wild smile stretches over his face. He even whoops and pumps his fist in the air.

"Dude. You scored! Awesome, man." Tyler comes across the room for the sole purpose of handing Nate an imagined post-coital high five.

This is my life now.

He looks over at me. "And hey, uh, good for you too. Nate's a really good lay. So I've been told."

Tyler then high-fives me as well. Aw. That's . . . equal opportunity, I guess.

"We actually. We didn't. Not yet. I mean." Nate looks at me.

"Already. Not today. At least, if we're going by when the sun's up," I say, really adding a lot to this conversation. Tyler just looks stupefied.

"Wait, what the hell are you doing here?" Nate asks his friend. "Aren't you supposed to be checking up on the chuppah?" He frowns. "Come to think of it, I should be there too. Fuck." He closes his eyes.

"Naw, man. Mike and Stacy are cool. Their parents are, like, super into the whole organizing thing, so we've just got to show up. No worries!" Tyler finger guns at Nate and laughs.

"Then is there a reason it's two in the afternoon and you're walking around without a shirt on? Or pants?"

Nate asks. We both stare down at Tyler's cute little boxers. They have sailboats on them.

He laughs, sounding a little embarrassed. "I, ah, met up with one of the romance convention ladies. Tigers. All of them." He even *rawrs* at me.

Sometimes I don't know what kind of alien world Tyler came from, but it must be fitfully amusing there.

"Nice. Who? Anyone I know?" I tease.

To my surprise, Tyler blushes. Actually blushes.

"Maybe. I mean. Sure?" He sighs. "One of your friends."

Oh my God, him and Shanna? I mean, they definitely had some prime time flirting going on last night, but I didn't imagine—

"There's my fucking star," Meredith says, walking out of the bedroom in her stocking feet, a cigarette clamped between her lips. She buttons up her cream blouse and shrugs on her beige jacket. She smiles at me. "The fuck are you doing here, gorgeous? You're supposed to be at your signing." Meredith puts out her cigarette in an old, left-over cup of coffee. She blows smoke, hands on her hips. "Jesus, we gotta get you moving."

Oh crap. Oh shit. Oh woe. Oh fuckmuppets. Between the wedding and my panel appearances, this happy little adventure has come at the worst possible damn time.

"Jesus, the signing," I groan, grabbing my purse and laptop case. Nate and Tyler both stand to the side, looking like they have no idea what is happening or what to do. Which is pretty much exactly the truth.

"I'll come with you," Nate says, hands in his pockets.

"Like, I'll just wait here," Tyler says, sounding lost.

"Good idea, sweetie. Go tuck yourself back into bed and I'll be around soon to fuck you good night." Meredith winks at him, and Tyler blushes again.

What the hell is happening to my life? I point to each of them in turn.

"Meredith, ew. Tyler, thanks. Nate, you don't have to come with me," I say as he goes over to the dresser, pulls out a new T-shirt, and throws it on. There is a brief flash of him in all his shirtless glory, which does a number on my heart. And, you know, other body parts. Then he's dressed. He even takes my laptop for me. Aw. Chivalry ain't dead.

"We, ah, need to take care of that business together. Later," he tells me.

We ignore Tyler's grunting enthusiasm. Not like that, dude. Well. Maybe like that. But look, we need to know if it's single fucking or married people fucking. Because if it's the latter, I may be too sick to my stomach to have an orgasm.

"Okay. Come to the signing, do the meet and greet, watch me shake some hands and ink some books. Then we'll go," I tell him. Meredith's already shoving me out the door.

"I'm so proud of you, kid," she grunts in my ear. Nate comes after us, holding my case.

"I'm kind of intrigued, since hearing you read last night. I want to see what the fuss is," he says, smiling.

Meredith waggles her eyebrows. "I like a man who likes a show," she says.

We walk, and I can't help the slight fluttering nervousness in my stomach.

Hopefully, Nate thinks we're a good crowd.

It kind of makes me wonder why I care what he thinks.

19

NATE

I'VE NEVER BEEN SURROUNDED by this many women in my life. I had no idea Julia was so popular. The line for her signing stretches across the carpeted ballroom floor, winding around several booths. I can see her up at the table, alongside two other women. She's laughing, chatting, tossing her hair. Something she says makes the woman she's signing for burst into raucous laughter. Julia's good at putting people at ease.

"Oh my God, I love this. I so rarely see dudes in this kind of line," a woman behind me says. She grins up at me, a pile of books in her arms. She's got curly black hair and dark skin, and wrinkles her nose as she studies me. "You sure you're in the right place, hon?"

"I love romance novels," I say, as neutrally as possible. Hopefully, I sound like I'm telling the truth. Playing along with other people's assumptions can be part of a lawyer's job. "This series with, ah, all the sex. Fantastic. Can't get enough."

"Wow. This is so weird," the woman says. She laughs,

and even slaps me on the arm. "I love it. Good for you, man."

"Thanks," I say, bemused as a couple of other ladies turn to gawk at me, like I'm some kind of mythological creature on display, a manticore reading Nora Roberts.

The line moves forward a bit, then halts, and I stop short. The woman from behind bumps into me, spilling her books. I pick them up for her. Damn. She's been balancing—five, six—*eight* paperbacks.

"Let me hold onto some of these until you get to the front," I tell her. She makes a gasping noise of relief. "Would've thought you'd have a tote bag or something. That's one thing I've noticed about publishing conferences; they give away totes like they're candy or something."

It's true. I saw a woman with five bags slung over her arms, who then ran to grab another free tote at the Ballantine table. Some mysteries I will never understand.

"Mmm, totable candy," the woman laughs. She nods. "Yeah, I always get too many books. It's my big problem. I mean, I read like crazy. Makes my morning commute easier. Sci fi, fantasy, thriller, you name it. Sometimes I pick up whatever Oprah tells me to. But romance is kind of my main passion. No pun intended." She grins. "Too many books. So yeah, not enough totes in the world."

"Maybe I can snag you one at the front, get it autographed. I know the author," I say.

The woman gasps and claps her hands over her mouth. It's kind of fun, being the one with the inside track. It feels like I know a celebrity. Hell, maybe I do.

"How do you know Julia?" the woman asks, suddenly turning coy. I play along, lifting an eyebrow.

"I know her very well," I tell the woman, leaving a hint of suggestion in my voice.

The woman giggles and even blushes. Christ, I need to tell Tyler about romance conventions.

"Maybe she based one of her alphas on you. Rolph Armani, maybe." She really seems to like that idea.

But . . . Rolph *Armani?* I can't help barking out a laugh.

She giggles as well. "Yeah, I know. Some of the names are kind of ridiculous. But isn't that half the point? It's a fantasy, after all. Like, if I met a guy on the street named Clint Embers, I'd know he was either a hustler or a wrestler. But in fiction? Totally normal."

"Right," I say, moving up the line and still carrying her books.

I'll admit it; I'd sort of imagined Julia signing books for a bunch of sad, lonely housewives who've never held a job in their lives and need someone to fix all their problems. You know. Someone who thinks the names Rolph Armani or Clint Embers belong to actual human beings. But as I chat with the woman—Maria, as she introduces herself—I see my idea was pretty mean-spirited. All right, I'll say it: idiotic. Maria's a pharmacist who rock-climbs in her spare time. Corinne, who's right ahead of us and couldn't help overhearing the conversation, introduces herself as a forensic scientist. Like Maria before her, Corinne is dumbstruck by my presence and all but starts prodding me to make sure I'm real and not a hallucination. It turns out that having a young man in this signing line is kind of like finding the Holy Grail, if the Holy Grail had a penis.

Women are peering at me, looking sideways or

standing on tiptoe. And a lot of them seem to already know each other.

"Look, I'm kind of over the whole billionaire thing," Maria says, offering me a gummy peach ring. I decline, and she chews thoughtfully. "Like, I get kind of tired of the over-the-top wealth porn. But that's why Julia's books are so amazing. She gives you the old clichés, the ones you think you're going to hate. You know, the one where the girl has to pretend to be the billionaire's secretary to get information for the cops, and then he becomes her Dom, all that kind of stuff. Except that her characters have, like, actual quirks of their own. One of her Doms was really into collecting, like, vintage Pogs from the 90s. And her women are all ballsy."

"Not a lot of damsels in distress," I say as we head up to near the front of the line.

Maria actually laughs at that. "Oh, hell no. Like, when I was reading my mom's Harlequin romances from the eighties, I read a lot of ladies crying in corsets or fainting in Monte Carlo or something. I know there's a place for all that, but it's not relatable anymore, you know? My husband can't afford for me to sit at home all day, and I wouldn't want to." She shrugs. "It's fine if that's what you want, but most of us can't afford that lifestyle."

"You're very action-oriented," I tell her.

Maria laughs. "Yeah, I'm all about action." She nudges me in a very wink-wink way. "That's probably what I like best about Julia: the sex scenes are fucking hot, man."

I laugh along with her, but she's absolutely right. The memories of last night are still a little hazy, but I distinctly remember growing hard as Julia read to me. It was the words, sure, but even better was how they were enhanced by the softness of her voice, the way she twirled her hair, the little smirk that graced her lips whenever she read something she thought sounded particularly good.

She's good at what she does, and she loves it. That's incredibly sexy.

Finally, we're at the front of the line. I deposit Maria's books on the table in front of Julia, but she's finishing up a conversation with a woman who's moved off to the side. The woman's crying, or has finished crying pretty recently. Her eyes are still watery, her cheeks red. Julia gives her a tissue. I notice she's holding on to the woman's hand.

"I'm sorry, I didn't mean to gush like that," the woman says, her voice soft and shaking. "I just wanted you to know how much it means."

"Trust me, I feel the same," Julia says, grinning. She's even wiping her own eyes now.

As the woman leaves, Julia looks up at me and waggles her brows. "A tall, dark stranger enters my midst. Anything in particular you want signed?" she asks, brandishing her pen. "Any parts?" Her eyes trail down my body, obviously landing on my crotch.

Maria starts laughing.

"I'm just the delivery system," I tell her, letting Maria up to the table. As Julia starts chatting with her fan, I side-step away. I find myself next to the crying woman, whose tissue is, by now, mostly used up.

"Dammit," she says, sighing. "I'm still all smudged."

I hand her another tissue. Apparently I'm now tissue guy. Hell, there are worse ways to live.

"Thanks." She sniffs, grabbing one.

"Are you, ah, all right?" I ask.

"I got a little overemotional. I do that sometimes," she says, smiling as she finishes wiping her face. "I just went through a really terrible divorce."

"I'm sorry," I say. It's an automatic response, but I find that I mean it, too. I feel oddly guilty, all of a sudden. Why does my business have to be so damn lucrative?

"Thank you." She wipes under her eyes again, and keeps talking. "He told me I was too fat for him. When we were signing the final papers, he told me I'd never find anyone to love me the way I am."

"Christ," I say, feeling like I walked into something I shouldn't be seeing. I also kind of want to punch this asshole in the face. Who says that kind of shit? Even during divorce?

Yesterday, I would've been faintly disgusted by this woman for telling me these sordid personal details. Right now, I just feel damn sorry for her.

"Oh crap, is this too much? I just launch into—" she says, pausing to blow her nose.

"It's fine," I tell her. She looks back to Julia, and so do I. Julia's about finished with Maria's books, grinning and laughing while they talk.

"I was telling Julia that her Abby Mills series, the one with the plus-size heroine, gave me the strength to get back out there. And I met a wonderful guy," she says, her voice cracking a little. She stops and waves her hands. "I'm sorry. You don't want to hear this." She flushes a little.

"No. Good for you," I tell her. And I mean it.

So Julia makes people laugh, makes them feel good about themselves, and helps them have fun. Why the hell was I giving her such a shitty time before?

I step away and watch her work. I watch her sign, giggling wildly at something another fan tells her. She even puts her head down on the table with laughing. She's free, happy, smart, talented . . . and maybe that's everything I didn't like about her at first.

After Phoebe left me, I didn't want anyone else, ever again. I told myself it was because I didn't want another woman wrecking my life, lying to me, cheating on me. The truth is, I didn't want to look into another woman's eyes—a woman I thought was spectacular, funny, smart, strong—and see that I didn't measure up.

But somehow, I'm starting to shed that fear. Julia looks over at me as her signing line finally begins to die down. She rests her cheek on her hand, and mimes going to sleep. She's playful, and she winks at me.

For fuck's sake, Nate. You need to find out if you're married or not.

The cool, lawyerly reserve comes over me as I check my phone. Shit. Only a few hours until Mike and Stacy's wedding. We need to go. God, we still don't even have any idea where this chapel is. Why can't—

"There are a ton of single ladies in this line," Tyler crows, coming over and grabbing me by the shoulder. "Dude, you hook me up with all the best places."

Of course Tyler figured out that romance conventions are full of women. I should never have underestimated his horniness.

He's wearing his shirt unbuttoned halfway, his sunglasses riding on top of his freshly gelled hair. He smells like bamboo body spray. It's not a great smell.

"I'm surprised Meredith let you out of the room," I tell him, looking back at Julia. Tyler whistles.

"Had to sneak out, bro. I was so hungry. We worked up an appetite." He sticks his tongue between his teeth and nods suggestively. "We had room service, but it wasn't enough. Oysters. Not my favorite thing." Then he continues scanning down the line of women, surfing with his eyes. He whistles. "Like, a bunch of sevens and eights riding along. I'm impressed. Hot chicks like to read."

"What the hell are you even still doing here? The restaurant's downstairs," I say. I'm even starting to snap at Tyler. Maybe because he's distracting me from focusing on the problem at hand. Find the wedding chapel, see if there's a marriage certificate.

Or maybe I'm irritated because he's distracting me from Julia. *Oh, fuck me.*

"Nothing wrong with scoping out the competition. Even if Meredith's like, super good in bed. Older chicks, man." He nods, like he's giving me some sage wisdom. The Tao of Tyler. "Older chicks."

Finally, the signing line ends. Julia stands up, talking to the other authors. They come over to us. She smiles at me, but not seductive. It's all business right now. Which is the way it has to be. Business. The way I want it to be.

Don't I?

"Ladies," Tyler says, walking over to Julia's friends, both attractive young women. Jesus fuck, is he flexing? "You had great form out there. Really good signing technique."

"Thank you?" one of the women says, looking to Julia with a comical expression.

Tyler doesn't seem to notice. He pulls out a card. Right, one of his "sexual professional but-not-in-a-gigolo-way" cards. He hands them out to all potential bed partners. I don't know how he ever manages to get laid. There used to be a picture of him on the back, with his shirt off and his skin tanned. I'm glad he removed it. Ruins the class factor of giving women your "come fuck me" phone number.

"Call me anytime," he says. Julia looks at me with wide eyes.

"Someone's a go-getter," she murmurs out the side of her mouth. "Hope Meredith doesn't mind."

"Um, baby, this isn't you," the woman says, scrunching up her face in amusement and handing the card back to Tyler. "Unless your last name is Presley."

"Oh shit," Tyler says, laughing as he takes the card back. "Sorry. Where the hell'd I get this from?" He whistles. "Must've found it in my room."

Wait a minute. "Presley as in Elvis?" I ask, snatching the card back from Tyler. Julia looks it over with me, and there it is, plain as daylight. Viva Las Vegas chapel, just down the Strip.

"That place looks awesome for anyone who wants to be my baby mama tonight," Tyler says, grinning as he tries to slip his arms around the two women. They each carefully dodge out of the embrace. Right now, his friendly douchebaggery is the least of my problems.

"Let's go," I tell Julia. She nods, grabbing my arm and dragging me away while Tyler protests.

"I already texted for an Uber," she says, starting to sprint down the hall. "The game is afoot!"

Not sure this mystery is quite Sherlock Holmes level. But as I chase after her, I have to admit something to myself: I don't want to let her go.

Fuck.

20

JULIA

I HAVE NEVER BEEN SO CONFLICTED about an answer
before in my life. At least, not since Bobby Carmichael
sent me a note in sixth grade asking to be my boyfriend,
and I had to decide if him having a Sega Genesis made up
for the fact that I thought he smelled like applesauce.

All right. Maybe preparing to discover whether I'm
married to a guy I've known less than twenty-four hours
isn't exactly the same as "Segagate." But it's close.

The cab pulls up right outside of a kitschy little chapel
at the very edge of the Strip. It's a cute little place, one
story, painted white with pink, heart-shaped shutters by
the windows. A plastic garden with Astroturf waits inside
a little white picket fence. There's a glowing neon sign at
the front, complete with Elvis himself, in glorious glittery
lights, gyrating above a sign advertising to Viva Las Vegas
in matrimonial bliss.

"Does your mouth taste like dust?" I ask Nate. He
looks a little sweaty, like he's not sure he wants to get out
of the car.

"A little, maybe. I thought that was because of the desert," he says, getting out and handing me out after him. Who says chivalry is dead? My possible-maybe-husband is a true gentleman.

We walk into the chapel, and I have to ask myself: would it be so bad being married to this guy?

Okay, leaving aside the fact that we don't know each other and Mom will flip the hell out, we've got the sexual chemistry thing under control. Like, it's very under control. It's in a safety deposit box at the bank under control. I have the key to it in my bra, tucked right up against my left breast.

Okay. Stop stalling, Julia. In we go.

We walk into a blast of air conditioning so frigid it freezes the sweat on my body, creating a really uncomfortable sensation. Around us, enough bouquets of pink and white roses have been arranged to supply three Italian funerals. Organ music blasts over speakers. It takes me a minute to realize that the music is a bunch of Elvis hits refigured for pipe organ. How nice. There's *Hunka Hunka Burning Love*; never thought I'd hear it as composed by Bach.

"Are you sure this is the right place?" Nate asks, looking around with a tight expression on his face.

I'm sure we're where we need to be, studly perhaps-husband. I hold up the card; the name is right there, in perfect gold foil.

"All right, let's get some answers," I say, and push open a pair of white painted doors . . . right into the wedding chapel, where two guys are in the process of getting married. They're in matching powder blue tuxedos, and one of them is weeping. With joy, I hope.

"Ah now pronounce you—" Elvis stops in the middle of his pelvis-thrusting wedding officiation to look up at us.

He's 1970s Elvis to the max, with a sparkly white rhinestone suit and a wig of perfectly coiffed, jet black hair. He takes off his gold-rimmed sunglasses.

"Can I help you?" he asks, dropping his voice to its normal register and looking like he's been on the clock for way too damn long. He pulls a hip flask out of his suit and takes a quick swig.

Everybody's working for the weekend.

"We're, ah, looking for our license," I say.

Elvis slides his glasses back down his nose. "Then you want Connie over at reception. Obviously," the guy finishes, muttering under his breath.

Elvis is a bitch.

"We're getting married!" the sniffly guy yells. He looks so proud. Aw, sweetie.

"Yay!" I cry out, giving them an enthusiastic thumbs up. They beam at me.

"Mazel Tov," Nate mutters, and we shut the doors, turning away from the chapel and back to the front desk. "You handle weird situations a lot better than me," he says.

I do believe he may be impressed.

"That'll be a good quality to have when we move into your condo," I say. Then I hold up my hands when he blanches a little bit. "Kidding. We really should pick our honeymoon destination, though. I'm thinking Cabo or Venice. One is more beach, but the other is more pasta. Can't decide."

Nate laughs at that, and rings the desk bell. He waits,

then does it again thirty seconds later. Again, a man who knows how to get what he wants.

I lean on the counter next to him, our arms against each other. A whisper of electricity brushes up my skin; I'm getting goosebumps just from his presence. Or maybe that's the air conditioning.

"Can I help you?" a woman asks, coming up to the counter from the back room. She's snapping gum, and has her hair poofed up in June Carter-style fabulousness. "Would you like our premium or deluxe package? Deluxe means you get to keep the rings. Here." She reaches under the counter and pulls out a black velvet tray with rhinestone sparklers in it. "Personally, I like the one with the swan-shaped diamond. It screams eternal bliss." She blows a bubble; the bags under her eyes tell me she might be pulling a double shift.

"We need to check our license. We might have gotten married here last night," Nate says, all business. The woman snorts.

"Might have? How blitzed were you, sweetie?"

Nate grumbles and takes my phone, showing her the picture.

She nods. "Yep. You had Daryl, our midnight Elvis. Good job, too. He's way more fun than Kyle. You know, the one officiating right now?" She sighs and picks at a scab on her finger. "Kyle drops character all the time. Daryl even takes his lunch break like Elvis. Peanut butter banana sandwiches and everything."

"That's . . . committed," Nate says at last.

"Yep. It'll kill him someday. Just like how Elvis died, trying to take a shit." She shakes her head. "It's what

Daryl wants. Anyway, let me get the license." She turns around and goes in the back.

I start nervously rapping my fingers on the counter. It wouldn't be so bad, would it? My leg starts jittering, and Nate lays his hand on top of mine.

"Whatever happens . . . we'll be okay," he says, squeezing my fingers.

I'm sure he means it in the "we'll be able to get a quickie divorce" sense, but maybe not. Maybe we could try it out for a while, see if the shoe fits. After all, I'm still reveling in memories of our lovemaking last night, and my toes curl even thinking about it.

I smile up at him, wanting to run my fingers across the fine stubbled line of his jaw.

He looks down at me, too. "Julia," he says. "I want—"

"Found it," Connie says, shoving back in through the door and slapping a piece of paper on the counter. "Congratulations. You are married in the great state of Nevada. Hope you have a long and happy life together."

She's still chomping on that gum, looking from Nate to me like she's anticipating three months before the divorce, tops.

I think my entire body's gone numb. I'm . . . married. Again.

"Wow," Nate says. It sounds like the wind's been taken out of him. He clears his throat, puts his hand on the wedding license.

My heart is pounding a mile a minute. Okay. So we're married. This can be dealt with if we need to, you know, get a divorce. I don't think Nate would try to pull anything with my money like Drew did, and I think he knows me well enough to know I wouldn't do anything like that to him.

But what if . . . what if he wants to give our marriage a shot?

Because I've been thinking about it on the taxi ride over here, thinking about the knot in my stomach. Now I realize I wasn't worried because I was afraid we were married; I was a little nervous to think that we weren't.

Not to say that this is the way I really wanted or pictured anything, but we do well together, Nate and I. Don't we?

Look, maybe we can agree to play it by ear for a month or two. If in eight weeks we know it's a bust, we just go to the courthouse and file and boom, we're done. Not married.

But if eight weeks go by, and we like it, maybe we try eight more weeks. And then eight weeks after that. And then . . . .

I don't know why I'm suddenly feeling giddy with happiness. It's crazy to feel this way, but I kind of want to smile and kiss the crazy jerk. David Tennant is right along with me, hanging out in the back of my head, giving me a thumbs up.

"*Allons-y*, darling! It's perfect," he calls, twirling his sonic screwdriver. I don't mean that in the dirty way at all. Mostly.

I tilt my head up to Nate, my lips parting. "Maybe . . . " I say.

"Hold on. Look at this." His eyes light up, and he passes the paper to me. I study the wedding license, not quite sure what the hell he's talking about.

State of Nevada, Elvis, it all seems perfectly legal. And

then my eyes fall onto the name written beside *Bride*. It looked so natural at first, I didn't even question it. But of course.

It's not my name. It's Lola Sinclair's name. And right underneath, beside *Groom* . . . .

"Peyton Manning?" I say, looking up at Nate in bewilderment. He nods.

"The man is a fucking god. You can't blame me for wanting to be him for one drunken night, even in a Las Vegas wedding chapel." He says it all with an air of reverence.

"Our chapel is one of the finest in the city," Connie says, a lit cigarette now clamped between her teeth. She blows a smoke ring, then gets a can of Febreze from under the counter and disinfects the air.

Nate and I take a step away.

"What does this mean?" I ask him, heart hammering. He grins.

"It means this isn't legally binding. Lola Sinclair doesn't exist, and I'm obviously not Manning. We don't have to worry." He folds the license up, creating a perfect, crisp fold in the center. Exactly symmetrical. "We're free."

And that's exactly how he sees it. He breathes such a sigh of relief, it's almost hard not to take it as an insult. Strike that: it's pretty impossible not to take it as an insult.

"Well, glad you don't have to burden yourself with the divorce process," I say, stepping backward.

He lets me go; he's still too caught up in the bliss of not being married to a stranger. And hell, can I really give him shit about that? I don't think so.

"Come on. We both would've been adults about it," he says, finally looking at me with an expression that suggests being eternally bound to someone after a night of hot sex *isn't* the best way to go about things.

Christ, I really was thinking this through like one of my books, wasn't I? Two strangers wind up in bed together after a night of pounding back shots and discussing heartbreak. They accidentally marry, have a huge breakup near the end, and then realize they're madly in love when one of them is just boarding a plane for Austria. Then the groom races along the runway, the airport police tailing him in their car, as he tries to get to the plane window as it's taxiing and about to take off.

In my novel's version, the hero also doesn't have a shirt on, but that's more for aesthetic purposes.

Point is, I've been acting like this'll end in some magical, embracing moment between the two of us, as we resolve to live like a couple of crazy people and not worry about things like jobs, living in different states, friends, compatibility, you know. All that boring adult stuff.

Maybe I *have* been too caught up in my work. Maybe it'd be good for me to take a step back and remember that in real life, you don't find your soul mate in a strip club, waking up with nothing more than a tattoo and some blurry memories.

"You're right. We would've been adults." I hold out my hand. "So, partner. Crazy Vegas adventure. At least we get to check that off the bucket list, right?"

Nate blinks; he looks like he doesn't quite get it. But he nods slowly, shaking with me.

"Yeah. I, uh, would invite you back to the room if you want. But I've got the wedding in a few hours. Besides, you're probably just relieved how this all turned out."

He doesn't even make it a question. My gut tightens at

his words, but I don't betray my fabulous calm. So fabulous. Much calm. Wow.

"I've got to get going anyway. The conference is still in swing. I haven't done as much mingling as I should have," I say. We walk out the doors, back into the oppressive Vegas heat.

Oh man. Sweat starts trickling down my back again, instantly.

"I know you love to mingle. Mingling's your bread and butter," he says, maybe a little louder than he has to. I can tell the relief is just radiating off of him.

"Bread and butter's okay, I guess. I prefer champagne and Hostess cupcakes. You know. Both classy and common," I say, smacking him on the shoulder. I actually smack him.

He just nods, dialing up a cab. While he's doing that, another taxi happens to come along, and I hail it.

"Want a ride back?" I ask, hoping that he'll get inside, and we'll have a quiet conversation, and—

"Thanks. I think I have to get in touch with the guys. They're probably out looking for me," he replies.

Right. He does not want to have much more to do with me now that our insane sex-having, bird-napping adventure is over. I get into the car and smile.

"See you around," I say. He nods.

"See you, Julia." He looks back at his phone, distracted, shut off. He's finished with one problem; now on to the next.

And just like that, I drive away.

21

JULIA

THERE IS no reason for me to be feeling like I need to curl up into a ball and cry. I didn't do that during my divorce from Drew, and I sure as hell won't do it after my near-miss marriage to Nate. Instead, I will repeatedly roll the window up and down in this taxi while staring bleakly out at the Las Vegas Strip, like a motherfucking grown-up.

Traffic is at a total standstill. We're pretty much just sitting in this cab. I can see the glittering cityscape ahead of me, but at the moment we're still kind of trapped next to the Rio, with the enormous picture of Penn and Teller beckoning me from across the way. Much as I love a good atheist magic show, I'm not in the mood right now.

Damn, I could walk backwards and be at the hotel faster than this.

"'Scuse me. You know any side streets?" I ask the cabbie. He just shrugs.

"Unless you know how to handle this vehicle off road in the desert, I would suggest staying where we are," he says in a clipped, pleasant accent. I nod and sit there, watching the red electronic numbers tick up and up, showing the amount of cash I owe.

I kind of hoped I'd be sharing this cab back with Nate, laughing with relief at our fake marriage ceremony. We'd chat about Mike and Stacy's wedding, maybe agree to meet up for drinks later, you know, just casual . . . .

Any hope I'd had that we could work this out evaporated back there, when he said he'd catch his own ride. When he'd started looking at his phone and basically giving me the brush-off. Our adventure is over. And in the grand scheme of things, it could've been way worse. We didn't do too many illegal things. Granted, I think he should place an anonymous call to Phoebe and alert her about Chester or Eduardo or whatever the fuck that parrot's name is, but beyond that, nothing really bad was done.

Though I think I should probably send flowers to that kidnap adventure guy I kneed in the balls.

My phone buzzes in my purse. I pull it out, heart hammering, hoping it'll be Nate. But no, Shanna. I grab the call.

"Hey," I say. Man, even *I* hear how glum and listless that sounds.

"What happened?" she says. "Did dickhead break your heart?"

"We just found out that Lola Sinclair and Peyton Manning got married last night, so it's not quite as simple as we'd all like," I tell her.

There's a long pause on the other end.

"Care to repeat pretty much everything you just said to me?" Shanna says. "What's been going on?"

"Where are you?" I sigh, my temples throbbing.

"The Venetian, having some chocolate. The Grand Canal smells a lot like chlorine, but otherwise it's just like actually being in Venice. Only more fanny packs. Come on over, meet up with us. Meredith's here." Her voice turns whispery. "And I don't want to hear any more about her carnal adventures with the surfer dude wannabe, so if you could hurry this up I'd seriously appreciate it."

"Hold on." I tap the glass, and the cab driver rolls down his window. "On second thought, drop me here. I'll walk it." I hand him cash.

So there I am, walking along the Las Vegas Strip, making sure I don't trip over my wedges and fall off the concrete embankment and into traffic. The hot desert wind whips by, blowing my skirt up almost to around my ass. Some cars honk, and I flip them off sullenly, my heart not really into it.

Vegas is a place that's pretty damn transitory. One second you're under the Eiffel Tower, the next you're wandering along the Venice canals, until you head over to New York for some pizza and maybe Ancient Egypt for a nightcap. So many different times and places in one condensed area. It's not about permanence. It's the ideal city for a fling.

And that's what the night with Nate was. A fling. Anything more would've been stupid, like betting all your money on a killer blackjack hand. The house always wins. And if you happen to cheat the house, it gets security to pull you into a back room, put a bag over your head, and break your kneecaps until you admit you cheated.

I'm pretty sure there was a metaphor somewhere in this, but now all I want to do is watch *Casino* and *Ocean's*

11. Maybe on the plane ride home, when I'm too depressed to read.

Venice welcomes me with its fake but still impressive recreation of St. Mark's Square. I wander down a carpeted Grand Canal, passing gondolas that drift under the bridges, gondoliers serenading people who are too busy playing on their phones to notice anything. I duck into Tintoretto Bakery, a cute and cozy place with gleaming wooden floors, rustic painted walls, and the smell of butter and chocolate in the air. It's so mouthwatering I forget for a second that I'm supposed to be in a bad mood.

Shanna and Meredith have a table in the corner and wave me over.

Meredith looks at me over the rim of her glasses, like I'm a kid in school who's done wrong. "So. Fucking wasn't enough? Promise me you had a pre-nup," she tells me as I slide into a chair.

So we're going straight for first degree, I take it.

"We didn't," I start, and sigh, rubbing the heel of my palm into my eye. "You don't have anything to worry about."

"Promise me you used a condom. Or used the pre-nup as a condom," she says, adding three teaspoons of sugar to her espresso. "Because the last thing you need right now is fucking genital warts."

Someone hisses at us from over at another table, a family with two small kids. Meredith clears her throat.

Oh shit. This is going to end with someone being arrested and someone else probably being thrown into the canal.

"Save it. I've had all the drama I need today," I say,

grabbing her arm. "Now buy me chocolate because I want it and because I make you a lot of money."

Meredith nods, looking proud. "I knew I'd taught you well."

She waves for the waiter while Shanna rubs my shoulder. The look in her eyes is soft, full of concern.

"So what happened? He gave you the brush-off?" Her eyes harden a little. After she heard the kinds of things Drew was saying to me, it took me sitting on the phone with her for an hour to prevent Shanna from driving to his new apartment to give him hell.

I smile. "Don't worry, he's not the epic disaster of humanity that Drew was. It was adult, grown-up. You know. Grown-up-ish. We realized that there was nothing holding us together. We don't live in the same state. A couple of good lays doesn't guarantee you a lifetime of happiness."

"Maybe not, but it's better to start off fucking great than fucking awful," Meredith says conversationally. The mother at the other table makes a shushing sound, and Meredith shushes right back. "Do I have to sell my tits to get a waiter or what?" she mutters.

She definitely earns her fifteen percent commission.

"So there's no way you can work it out? You seemed into him," Shanna says, squeezing my hand.

I play with the sugar packets. Just leave me here with my sugar and Stevia friends, and we shall build a fortress together to guard against men and heartbreak and bitter coffee or something.

"I kind of left the door open, and he politely closed it and then shouted *no thanks* through it. Like I said, I can't blame him." I sigh and fiddle with the straps of my purse.

"Much as my motto towards men is 'fuck them, then eat them,' " Meredith says, looking in her compact mirror and adjusting her makeup, "I have to ask: do you think he could be doubting this whole thing as much as you are?" She snaps the case closed and looks at me, her eyeliner much better. "The only thing men fear more than professional catastrophe or debilitating illness is rejection. Maybe he thought he'd ask you on a date and that you'd turn him down. Nothing makes their testicles retreat into their bodies more than a woman giving them a pitying look and saying no. Weak little shits."

"You know, there is such a thing as reverse sexism," Shanna says flatly. "Some people pretend there isn't, but it exists."

I tune out their critique of third wave feminism for a little trip to my mind palace. This is where I get all of my most important thinking done. It's great here. I have every issue of the Dark Phoenix saga in mint condition. *The Great Mouse Detective* plays on a loop in the background. David Tennant and Chris Eccleston are letting me have this thinking moment on my own, mercifully.

Maybe Meredith's right. Maybe Nate just needs to know what's in my mind. And in my heart? Fuck, maybe. I haven't had these feelings in so long, since Drew gutted me and left me to get back on my feet and move on, alone. On the outside I looked fine, but inside, I was hollow.

I didn't mind, though. I mean, not much. The empty shell was held together with nothing more than strong will and a lot of root beer. But I don't want that to be my life, walking around with an invulnerable air and living alone.

So maybe . . . maybe if I just tell him the truth.

I don't want any hot chocolate now. I'm full of purpose, dammit.

The waiter comes over to me. I look up, ready to tell him no thank you, that I'm good, when his eyes light up.

"Oh thank God! It's you," he says, clapping a hand over his heart.

"Uh. Is this about last night?" I say sheepishly. Man, I really was a busy little rabbit, wasn't I? "If so, I'm sorry for anything I did or said or fondled."

The waiter waves his hand, dismissing it. "Don't even worry. It's Vegas. I've seen worse. But I'm so glad you're back. We were all super freaked out. Here, hold on." With that mysterious comment, he runs back to the counter and talks with the girl.

Shanna's eyes are wide. Meredith frowns. "You didn't leave a dildo, did you?" she asks.

"No," I snap. Then I do a quick mental inventory. I don't think we were missing one . . . .

"Here," the waiter says, returning with something in his hand. He places two gold wedding bands into my palm.

"My fake wedding rings," I say, trying not to roll my eyes. I give him a smile. "Thanks. Thought I lost them."

"Those are fake?" he asks, whistling. "If you don't mind me saying, those are way nice to just get for a gag. Engraved and everything." He turns and walks away, and my blood chills.

"Engraved?" I look inside the bands, and bam.

Sure enough, engraved right on the inside: *To Stacy, my love forevermore.* And in the other: *Mike, my heart is always yours.*

Oh, fuck me with a hamster wheel and don't even ask how that's physically possible.

"These are Mike and Stacy's," I say, running through the timeline in my head. Yep. Last night bachelor party, today hangover brunch, early afternoon getting ready, and the wedding . . . is happening soon. Right now. Oh shit.

"How the hell did this happen?" Shanna gasps, taking the rings and staring at them like they're about to explode in her hands.

"Nate's the best man. He must've had them on him, or we went back to the room, or . . . something!"

"What the hell were you guys doing with them?" Shanna asks.

"WATCH HOW FAST I can make it spin," Julia says, her glee written all over her face. Or maybe that's just 'cause her lipstick's all smeared.

Heh. Smeared.

Drunk you, I'm not fucked. See? I can drink my coffee. All the coffee. I drink some and it spills down my face. The sight of it makes Julia laugh really hard. The gold ring spins on the table, and it's pretty fast, but fuck it. I'm gonna spin it faster.

Vegas, baby!

"Think we could use these to bet at a blackjack table?" I ask her, her pretty pink face turning all blurry and fuzzy.

Heh. Fuzz.

"We should definitely try," she whispers.

The waiter comes over to us. Man, what's he got to look weird about?

"I love you. Have my babies!" Julia howls, falling at his feet and lying on the floor. She gurgles.

"Here's your bill," he says, handing it over with a nervous look on his face.

Heh, this asshole thinks I'm going to give him my card. I shove the rings in the bill thing and hand it back.

"Solid gold," I say, and go in for a high five.

23

JULIA

"NATE IS A BAD BEST MAN," I say, sitting there in rigid horror.

"Opportunity knocks. And when it doesn't knock, it kicks down the fucking door and robs you at gunpoint," Meredith says, gripping my hand. "This is your chance, kid. Go find that loser, give him the rings back, save the damn wedding, and then get him to eat your ass out in celebration."

The family of four just abruptly gets up and leaves. The mother shoots us a dirty look. I wince in apology.

"I'm with Meredith, though perhaps in the spirit rather than the detail," Shanna says, nodding. "Go. Save the day. And tell him how you feel. You never know."

I get up and race out of the restaurant, the rings in my purse, my heart in my throat.

It's true that you never know. It's not knowing that's the hardest part of all.

24

NATE

I AM FUCKED.

These are words I normally never say, never think. Even in the most painful, intense divorce litigation, I never flinch. I home in on the problem, disappear down a tunnel of alpha lawyer fucking awesome, because I am going to win this motherfucker. That is how I am. That is what I do.

And now, two goddamn wedding rings have thrown me so hard off my game I might as well pack the whole show up and head back to Chicago. I stand in the middle of the living room, the area around me looking like it's been struck by a very angry whirlwind.

I've been a terrible goddamn best man. I abandon my friend at his own damn bachelor party to get laid. Admittedly, I'm not too sorry about that part, but it's still a shitty thing to do. Then I spend most of the next day, the *wedding* day, running around the Strip looking for my almost wedding venue when I should've been sticking by Mike, helping him avoid Tyler's ridiculous pep talks. And now, when I've just managed to struggle into my best man suit, barely ready for the ceremony in time, with my tie undone and my hair looking like something nested in it, I can't find the specially engraved rings.

This is why I shouldn't have sex. I should just develop a polyp of myself, cut it off my body, and then grow it so it can go off and help other people get divorced. I'll loan it my best suit, hair gel, everything. The point is, no more sex. Ever.

All right, I can't hold to that. But back to the problem at hand. The couch cushions are all over the goddamn floor. Did I check the bedroom? Thoroughly?

I tear the bed apart, pull the comforter down, rip off the sheets. I shake out the pillows, crawl on my hands and knees across the bathroom floor, even check my contact lens case to make sure I didn't get creative with my placement last night.

Last night. A lot of it's come back to me, but not all. Who the fuck knows when I'll remember everything else? Shit, maybe I dropped the rings in the fountain outside. Maybe I gave them to a hooker. Maybe I left them in Phoebe's house, and now she'll have an easy way to tie me back to breaking and entering—I broke into my ex-girlfriend's house, what kind of insane asshole am I?—and I can kiss my entire goddamn life goodbye.

Most of all, I'll ruin my fucking best friend's wedding, and why? Because motherfucking tequila, that's why. Because I am a shitty asshole friend, that's why.

Why is it every shitty romantic choice starts with a shot of tequila? Why can't it be gin, just once, for fuck's sake?

While I'm lying on my stomach and studying every inch of the carpeted living room floor, the door opens.

Fuck me. Mike.

He comes inside, doing up his cufflinks. He even put the stupid boutonniere in his lapel. It's a purple orchid with a spray of glitter. Stacy thought they were the best. Her whole bouquet is made up of orchids.

Can you get married if you don't have rings? Can we get them some ring pops, like in the proposal scene in *Deadpool?* Will I have to carry them down the aisle clenched in my ass, just like in *Deadpool?* Why the fuck am I thinking about *Deadpool* so much? Besides the fact that that movie is perfect, I mean.

Mike grunts when he sees me trying to do the worm across the living room. He looks around the destroyed area, the coffee table overturned, the pillows everywhere.

"Oh shit. Okay," Mike says, running over and kneeling beside me, gripping my shoulders. "Tell me the truth, buddy. How much coke did you snort?" He looks genuinely freaked. Even though I'm ruining his wedding, I swat him away impatiently.

"Christ, it's not like that. I'm . . . I'm checking the cleanliness of the place." I get back on my stomach and try to look around the coffee table debris.

Shit, if Julia were here now, what would she think?

And now I have to stop thinking about Julia, because the last thing I need is an accidental boner when I tell my friend I've sabotaged his wedding.

"I'm pretty sure you have better things to do in the fifty-seven minutes before I get married," Mike says, though he just sounds kind of puzzled. "What the hell's going on with you?"

Maybe if I pretend to have amnesia. No. Even *I* think that's fucking lame.

"Why don't you go downstairs and keep Tyler from getting laid in the chocolate fountain? I'll just be up here getting ready," I say, checking under the couch.

Oh, there's something under here. I reach under and come up with two mint Life Savers. Fucking mint. No one eats that anyway. Whose are these?

"You have a distinct aura of shitting-your-pants-in-terror going on right now. As you're the best man, I would think our positions would be reversed. Like, maybe I start freaking out and you give me an inspiring speech about love. Well, not inspiring, because it's you," Mike says, sitting on the couch and glaring down at me.

I get up, straightening my jacket. This is what I need to do: adopt glacier Lawyer Face™ and tell him that the rings are no longer in my possession. This is not an admission of guilt; it's simply stating that at some point last night, the rings left my possession, potentially by thievery or a third party. If that is the case—

"I lost your wedding rings, man." Who am I kidding? Even I'm not that big a dick. I can't even look Mike in the face right now. "I got really drunk last night, and I can't remember everything yet. I don't know where they are."

Christ, I have to turn around. I put my hands in my pockets and walk over to the window, gazing at the Strip as the sun starts setting right behind the mountains. The whole city is bathed in dusk and deep red, the lights starting to glint on the desert horizon. "I'm sorry," I mutter.

"Is that it?" Mike asks, walking over to stand next to me. He looks out at the mountains with me. No big emotion in his voice, no incredulous shouting about how I could possibly be this dumb. Just two guys looking out at some motherfucking mountains. "Shit. I thought it was an emergency, like you were sick or you kidnapped Liam Neeson's daughter."

"Oh shit. Now I remember," I say, widening my eyes. Mike smiles.

See? I'm hilarious.

"Well, you can give her back. Probably." Mike finally does glance at me. "It's okay. No big deal. We'll find a replacement set, or we'll mime it or something."

"It *is* a big deal, Mike. I know how much those rings cost you. I'll pay you back for it," I mutter. It'll suck to hell and back, but I'll do it.

"Look, is this the most thrilling thing to hear on my wedding day? No," Mike admits. "But you know what's pretty damn thrilling? I'm getting married to the woman I love more than anything else in this world." He says it slowly, like I'm an alien who's only recently started learning English and he's trying to instruct me. "I've got my best friends beside me. Even Tyler, overgrown toddler though he is, is important to me. This is what matters, man. Not the rings, or the venue, or the glow-in-the dark dildos from the girls' bachelorette party." He lifts his eyebrows. "Though I think Stacy snuck a couple into her luggage for the honeymoon."

"I liked it better when you were mad at me," I say, throwing up a little in my own mouth.

"I was never mad at you, Nate. I love you, asshole." He slaps my shoulder. "Stacy will probably flip out a little more about this than me, but I know she'll be okay.

Because us being together is what we've both been waiting for and building up to."

"How do you do it?" I ask him. I can't stop myself; I have to know. "How do you know that this is the right thing? Besides the fact that you guys've been shacking up for the better part of a decade. And Stacy's Alabama family wanted to take a shotgun to you five years back."

"You forget the part where Uncle Aaron is actually packing heat at the ceremony." Mike shrugs. "I don't go in for a lot of flowery language, you know me. But how do you know you found the one?" He counts on his fingers. "You have more fun with her than you do on your own. Everything's an adventure. You're compatible in the ways that matter. The sex is hot. And you trust that she'll be next to you, no matter what happens." He shrugs. "That's the reason to get married, man. That's the only reason. I mean, now that we don't have to marry for property or shit."

"Stacy would probably be happy to bring a couple of goats into the household," I say. "You know, for tradition's sake."

"I was thinking more a milk cow, but yeah. Same principle," Mike replies.

I laugh a little, because who doesn't love a good livestock joke? But I'm also thinking now. Because what Mike says about adventures, having fun, trust . . . . Every word he says projects Julia's face even more into my mind.

During all my years with Phoebe, we made logical sense. We enjoyed the same movies, had the same job, liked the same things in bed. But there was always something missing, and when I look back now, I understand why she left. She wasn't complete. Whole. She was content, maybe, but happy? Probably not.

For the first time, I realize it wasn't about *me* not measuring up. It was about *us* being the wrong fit.

As much as she can infuriate me sometimes, I know that no one has been able to make me smile or laugh like Julia. Even if we hadn't spent the day dealing with Elvis clones or fighting off pseudo Soviet kidnappers, it would've been fun.

I get a flash of a memory, the two of us in a café, probably way early this morning. We were laughing, and I remember the feeling I had in my gut. It was almost giddiness, a kind of relief. With Julia, there's nothing to worry about. Even when we want to kill each other, it's easy.

And I closed the door on our potential relationship. I shut down when we found out the certificates were false. I shut her out as fast as I could. There were excuses, in my own head, for why I was doing it. It didn't seem like the right thing at the right time. After all, we live in different cities, different states. Who wants that kind of a negotiation headache after one night in Vegas? Absolutely no one.

Most of all, there was the fear of seeing the same disappointment in her eyes that I saw in Phoebe's when it was over. I don't want that pain ever again.

But what if it's right? Isn't it worth every pain if it's right?

Shit. I sent her back to the hotel on her own.

But she didn't seem all that interested in being married to me either. She could've said something, done something.

Maybe that was her grand romantic moment of waiting. Maybe she wanted me to sweep her off her feet, like the characters in her novels. And I didn't measure up. Again. I had the chance, and I fucking fumbled the ball.

"You okay, dude? You're looking a little glassy-eyed all of a sudden," Mike says, sounding kind of worried.

I sigh, straighten my tie, and button my jacket. It's show time. "We should probably be heading down. They don't like for people to be late to the grand patio. At least, by *they*, I mean Stacy's parents. They're the ones who booked the venue."

"Yeah, but my parents paid for the decorations and the lights. Pretty sure they rent everything by the hour, so we'd better move our asses," Mike says.

We head in the elevator, ride down to the ground floor. My stomach's still twisted in fucking knots. Though whether that's because of the rings or Julia, I don't have a clue.

We walk out, head right and run toward the patio. I can see a couple of Stacy's bridesmaids headed that way as well. Their pale purple taffeta dresses blow around in the hot desert wind as we get outside. I should be doing normal bachelor best man shit, scoping out their asses, trying to figure out which one'll be open to fucking in the veranda after the ceremony. But I'm just not into it.

Because they're not Julia. She's not standing there at the entrance to the patio, wearing a pretty yellow dress, her hair done up and the rings in her hands and—

Actually, that is exactly what's happening. All of it. I run up to her, every muscle in my body awake and alert. She looks up at me. A strand of her hair floats across her mouth. I want to pull it away, slow and sexy like, and ask—

"Do you guys want to get married today or what?" Julia says breathlessly, looking over my shoulder at Mike. "If so, I got what you need. And for the right price, it can be yours."

She holds out her hand, the golden rings glinting in the fading sunlight. She smiles at me, but her eyes dart away fast. She doesn't want to act like she sees me; probably doesn't want to make things more awkward than I left them. I take the rings from her, wanting to sound collected, like I've got my shit together.

Instead, "I thought I was going to pass out." I clear my throat. Idiot. "Where were these bad boys?" I sound much better, cool, unruffled. Like it's every day that I leave my best friend's wedding rings in . . . the strip club?

"The café at the Venetian. We got some killer croissants at some point between bird-napping and the fountain."

"We washed our hands before we ate, right?"

That's not a joke; my stomach just rippled at the thought.

Julia shrugs. "Let's hope we remember. Or maybe, let's hope we don't."

"There you are!" Stacy runs at us, looking admittedly stunning in her strapless wedding dress. Her veil floats behind her, and I think I can actually see cartoon hearts in Mike's eyes. Stacy hugs Julia, then looks at me. "I didn't know where you were! What is this?"

"We, ah, that is, I," I stammer, trying to think of a way to spin this. Mike's no fucking help, still sitting there in a Vegas fairy tale staring at his perfect soon-to-be wife.

"You saved the wedding, didn't you?" Stacy asks Julia, taking the rings. "You're my hero, lady. Great job, Nate." She winks at me, clearly not mad, and hands them back.

"Hold onto these for the next fifteen minutes. Can you do it?"

"Yes," I say, feeling chastened. She's got a right to tease.

"You. You're going to be in the wedding," she says, pulling at Julia and practically dragging her behind. Julia almost trips on the bridal train.

Good, because I wasn't sure how else this was going to be fucking ridiculous.

"Do I get a choice?" Julia asks, throwing a glance over her shoulder at me. Does she want a rescue? Or maybe she wants to make sure I'm following.

I don't want that idea to please me as much as it does.

"Only thing is you have to be on the groom's side. Tyler just came down with a raging case of stomach sickness. Last I heard, he was throwing up everything he ever ate." Stacy sighs. "I was going to get Uncle Aaron to stand in his place, but he'd insist on keeping his Uzi strapped to his back. I'd prefer someone without ammunition."

"Tyler's sick? What happened?" I ask, alarmed.

Stacy laughs, airily waving her hand. "His sugar mamma took him to get oysters. Apparently one of them disagreed with him."

Julia Stevens and her friends: the source of all my frustration and happiness on this trip.

As the afternoon slides into evening, we get into our positions and walk up the aisle. A singer is crooning at the microphone, there are rose petals scattered at our feet as we walk up to the rabbi, then move to the side.

Soon, we're standing next to each other, Julia right up beside me. I can smell her perfume, and it's intoxicating. Everyone settles down and waits. A moment later, Stacy walks up the aisle on her father's arm, beaming at everyone.

And all I want to do is reach out, just put a hand through the air, and touch Julia. I want to feel the strap of her dress, the smooth skin underneath.

But I can't. Because this is someone else's wedding. And I can't say a fucking thing.

25

JULIA

A COUPLE of things flit through my mind as I watch Stacy walk down the aisle.

First: I hope Meredith's okay. Because I warned her not to order seafood in the desert, and she never listens to me.

Second: Stacy is a gorgeous bride, and Mike looks so radiantly in love with her that it even makes me, professional romance writer, a little sick to my stomach. But mostly sick with happiness.

Third: I absolutely cannot look at Nate. Because if I do, with this whole fairytale wedding unfolding before my eyes, I might projectile vomit onto him due to nerves and crippling sadness. And I think Stacy and Mike have put up with enough weirdness from us today.

They're at the vows now.

"I, Mike, take you, Stacy, to be my partner in all things. I promise constant arguments followed by ecstatic make-ups. I promise to let you sleep in every other day when I make breakfast, but I'm expecting French toast on Tuesday and Thursday."

Ah, so they wrote out their vows. Stacy laughs at a lot of parts that I don't even get; couple inside jokes. In some ways, that's what I miss most with Drew. Being silly with each other, laughing about things that other people didn't even get.

Maybe that's when I knew our marriage was over, six months before he walked out. Because the laughter had dried up.

And with Nate next to me, that momentary blip of closeness that I felt with him for the first time in so long, I start to tear up. Not because it was hot—although it was —or because it was swooningly romantic. I felt something I swore I wouldn't be able to feel again. That closeness, that fun, that intimacy. But it's over before it started. It's all fizzled out, and now I've got a bunch of memories distorted in an alcoholic haze, and nothing else.

Here's the nice thing about weddings: nobody wonders or makes an awkward face when you cry. A couple of hot tears slide down my cheeks, and I feel his hand on mine. Nate. I look up at him, daring to hope—

He hands me a tissue. Right. Don't want to smear the mascara and frighten the children. I dab at my eyes, and Stacy finishes her vow.

There's a bit where the rabbi finishes up, folds a napkin around a glass, and the happy couple breaks it underfoot. That must be the big moment, because everybody cheers, and Mike and Stacy kiss deeply.

Despite the ecstatic applause, I'd bet any money they don't hear us right now. They're probably caught up in the gloriousness of that moment, the one where they think it's going to go on forever. Nothing can damage them; nothing can get in the way.

And damn, I hope they're right.

"EVERYBODY GET OUTTA THE WAY. I need to nurse my agent's hangover," I shout, squeezing in between people on my way to the bar. Someone laughs as I find Meredith, still with an ice pack on her head, sitting with Tyler on the stool beside her.

They each have some fizzing glasses of ginger ale at hand, and look like people Edward Gorey would've drawn when he was feeling particularly malicious. *M is for Meredith, barfing her guts out. T is for Tyler, trying to get his nuts out.*

Or something. I'm not really a poet.

"Still not feeling it?" I ask them, knocking back some water. Hydration. It's important in the desert.

"I think I need to go to bed soon," Tyler says.

"Good. I'll join you," Meredith croaks. He actually smiles and tries waggling his eyebrows, but it doesn't completely work.

Of all Meredith's strange hook-up stories, this one is pretty near the top of the weirdness list. Well, everyone needs a little fun in their lives.

I meet up with Shanna out on the floor, where she's dancing with Brenda Summersby. Toni and Daphne, two of the other authors, are chatting with the DJ. One day, Mike and Stacy are going to have to explain to their kids why there were so many romance authors at their wedding. Where there is free cake and dancing, you can expect us to crop up. We're sort of like lemmings that way, only in wedge sandals.

"Sort of can't believe you didn't have the hook-up with Tyler," I say to Shanna, as we dance a little bit. She twirls me.

"Honestly, hair gel isn't really my thing. Besides, I, uh, kind of got a text from a certain person." Her eyes are particularly glowing right now.

I know she's been out on a few dates with someone from online, someone she was into, but . . . .

"They want to make it official?" I ask, feeling giddy with how giddy Shanna looks. She nods, and I squeeze her. Subtle as a Sphinx, this one. I never get *any* intel on who she's seeing until it's a serious thing. "Boy or girl?"

"Girl. Tabby. Enough about me," she says, pulling me off the floor a minute. She looks at me with what can only be described as loving concern. "Did you talk to him?" She gives me that look, the one that only your closest friends can give when they know exactly how sad you are because they have a damn laser vision.

I shake my head. "There's really nothing to talk about. He didn't get in the cab. The metaphorical cab, I mean. Well, the physical one too. So in that sense, it was sort of this metaphysical cab. Get it?" I wish Shanna would lighten up about my shitty philosophy jokes. They're great for parties, dammit.

"I swear, he's been throwing looks at you all night," she says.

I scoff. "No he hasn't. Has he?" I honestly wouldn't know. My eyes have a primary directive: look wherever Nate Wexler isn't.

My heart beats a little faster at the thought . . . . *No. Don't be an idiot, Julia.*

"Go talk to him," Shanna says, nudging me. She

glances across the room, where Nate is doing his best Grumpy Cat impression next to the buffet. "You'll regret it if you don't."

"Yes, I'll often wonder whatever became of the surly man of my dreams." But I squeeze her hand and walk away, over to Nate. He watches me with that glacier-smooth expression.

You could wreck the Titanic on that gaze.

"Hello to you, too," I mutter, standing beside him.

"Hello," he says.

Great. We've got the firing shots finished. Okay, who talks first? I guess it's me. Before I can get a word out, though, he says, "Do you want to take a walk?" He looks at me.

Damn, I wish that face weren't so unreadable. Or so damnably handsome.

I don't really wish that last part, actually.

"A walk to where? Out into the desert? I think I've done enough of that." But my heart's pounding, shaking, and kicking up its heels with glee. None of this is medically safe, by the way.

"Want to go to Paris?" he says.

I think he's being wildly spontaneous, and immediately my imagination explodes with vivid speculation. It'd be just like one of my books, where the hero has a private jet waiting and the heroine follows him to a romantic European destination, and they kiss and make love under the stars by the Seine, and then—oh. Hold on. He means the casino. Right.

"Sure," I say, going for super casual. "I have nowhere else to be." Nate doesn't respond to this. No, that'd be hoping for too much.

"We'd better hurry. They're about to start lifting them on chairs."

Actually, Mike and Stacy are firmly ensconced in chairs and being carried around the room by excitable family members by the time we leave. We walk out of the ballroom, heading out of the hotel and walking down the Strip.

"So what are you in the mood for?" I ask. "Pretty sure we can get champagne on the cheap. Though maybe we shouldn't have more booze."

"We don't tend to make the best decisions under the influence, no," he agrees.

And there you have it. Our whole tryst, if that's the word, was one big fat *not best decision*.

Honestly, why am I even going with this guy?

"Look, you just want to do this here on the sidewalk? My blister hasn't completely healed," I tell him.

Nate turns, looks at me a moment. The fountain comes on beside us, starting its elegant evening show. Nate steps around a group of photo-taking Japanese tourists and comes up to me.

"I just want to show you something. And then you don't have to worry about me anymore, all right?" he says evenly. I put my hands on my hips.

"I don't like being dragged around by a sullen dude."

"Fine." He puts a smile on his face; it looks like he's being forced under torture. "Does this look better?"

"Stick with surly. Stay with what you know," I grumble. Nate sighs and gestures to the lights of Paris ahead of us in the dark. I really would like to go inside, if only to take it all in.

"Can I buy you a drink?" he asks.

"What about the no alcohol policy?"

"One doesn't kill anyone."

"No, but one more might." I sigh, shrugging. "Fine. Let's go to Paris."

We walk silently the rest of the way. I have to admire the casino as we walk inside. They've painted the walls to resemble a blue sky over a lovely Parisian neighborhood. Inside the hotel, Nate leads the way to the Eiffel Tower. The bottom of it has been sculpted into the casino, and an elevator waits to take you up to the top, high above us in the Vegas sky.

"Where are we going?" I ask as we get inside the elevator.

"You'll see," he answers. I look at him, my eyebrows lifting. If he didn't have a heart attack level of seriousness on his face, I'd think that there was something wacky going on here.

The doors open, and we exit into the Eiffel Tower restaurant. The soft mood lighting and the tinkling piano music lend the diners a kind of romantic air. The windows look out onto the sparkling Las Vegas surroundings.

Nate speaks with the hostess, making sure to turn his back so that I can't hear. The lady nods and beckons me. "We have your table, sir."

Table?

I follow Nate to a small, private corner of the restaurant. It's a booth tucked into a little alcove, our own exclusive view out our own exclusive window. On the table, there's an incredible looking chocolate soufflé, strawberries and cream, and a chilled bottle of champagne waiting. Two glasses sparkle in the light. I gape, not making the world's most articulate noises.

Nate turns to me, and I watch the walls come down. His eyes are alive, questioning, claiming mine. I realize, with kind of a shock, that the poker face lawyer façade isn't just there when Nate is kicking ass. It might also be there when he's nervous. When something's important.

"Julia. I brought you here to ask you a very quick question." Nate takes my hands into his own. Then, slowly, he gets on one knee.

"Oh my God," I mutter, because this is way too much like the ending out of one of my books. After a misunderstanding and break up, the hero realizes he can't live without the heroine, and—

"Will you not marry me right now?"

System malfunction. Loss of data. Cannot speak. All your base are belong to us. What the what?

"You . . . want to . . . " I can't quite form the words.

Nate grins; a full, honest smile. "Please don't marry me right now. And if you choose to not marry me this moment, I can promise you an exciting future filled with very exciting headaches. Like travel. I know we live in different places, but they're not impossibly distant."

"You're in Chicago, I'm in Milwaukee. It's doable," I say.

Heh. Doable. Christ, pay attention right now.

"Besides the romantic possibilities of multiple Amtrak rides, I can offer you orgasms before breakfast, arguments over where to go to dinner, and a whole host of potentially erotic problems before lunch."

I like a man who plans around the day's meals. But I do have to be a little serious right now. Because when he presses his lips to my hand, gently, romantically, I nearly collapse in what I hope would be an attractive swoon. Every molecule in my body lights up.

"We barely know each other," I say, though I'm hoping that he'll say something about—

"I know, and it's crazy. It absolutely is." He looks into my eyes, a bemused smile playing on his lips. "If I were hearing about this from a friend, I'd be telling him to go to a shrink. But it didn't happen to my friend. It happened to me."

"What did?" I ask. I can barely breathe as he gets up, still holding my hands.

"I could be falling in love with you," he says, his lips mere inches from mine.

I close the last bit of distance, and I'm wrapped in his arms. The kiss sends the hot wash of feeling over me, the kind that makes me want to start ripping his clothes off. As per usual. But it's tempered with something else. Gentleness.

We pull apart, and he leans his forehead against mine. "It was something Mike said to me this afternoon. When you know you've found something that's right. This could be right. And I don't want to make what could be the mistake of my life because I was too goddamn scared." He touches my cheek. "What do you think?"

He could be falling in love. I close my eyes. "As crazy as it sounds, I could be feeling the exact same things," I say, kissing him again. We linger there a moment, and I almost hate when we break apart. "Any guy who orders chocolate soufflé gets in my *might love* book."

He wraps his arms tight around me and lifts me off the ground, just a little bit. I laugh, not minding when my feet leave the earth. I look up at him, bathed in the soft glow of the Las Vegas lights.

"So. Should we go back to the party?" he asks, beaming. The corners of his mouth lift, his eyes soften. I think he was as nervous and hopeful as I was.

I like that.

"In a couple of minutes. There's champagne, after all. I'd hate for all of it to go to waste," I say. Giggling, I slide into the booth, and he does the same.

WE WALK BACK DOWN the Strip, my arm through Nate's. I'm leaning against him, and he kisses the top of my head.

How can you want to kill someone and then never want them to ever leave you again, all within forty-eight hours? The emotional whiplash is killer. But I like it.

If I were writing this in a book, I would've had the happy ending nailed down tight on the final page, it's true. There would've been a definite proposal, a serious assurance to the reader that this is forever. No one likes open-ended stories.

But hey, this is actual life. Kidnappers in balaclavas, breaking and entering to steal a parrot, all real. And in real life, you may not know exactly how something is going to go. You may not know in twenty-four hours exactly how the story will end.

But you can have a pretty good idea.

"The Bellagio's beautiful at night," I say, as we stop outside the gate and look at the fountain. The colored lights are flashing, turning the water brilliant aquamarines and violets as the spray erupts into the air. Nate stiffens for a second.

"What?" I ask, startled. He smiles.

"I think I remember something," he says. Then he lifts my chin, and kisses me.

26

NATE

YESTERDAY, 5:30 AM

JULIA'S LAUGHING, and I don't remember why. All I know is it's the sexiest damn thing I've ever heard.

"Come on!" she shout-whispers, running toward the fountain.

Shit. Part of me is afraid of getting caught. The hornier part wants to know if she'll take her clothes off. Hornier wins out, as usual.

"We'll get in trouble," I say, walking toward her in a mostly straight line. Already she's shimmying out of her skirt and stepping out of her heels. Next thing I know, I'm peeling off my jacket and unbuttoning my shirt. No way she is doing her *La Dolce Vita* naked routine without me.

Julia dips a toe into the fountain, then steps in, shrieking a little at the cold. The fountain is quiet. The show probably doesn't start for another fifteen minutes or so. I get in after her, sloshing around behind her and grabbing her around her waist. She giggles, arching back against me and looking up into my eyes. I kiss her, running my hands along her breasts, down her body. She spins around and away from me, dancing a little.

"Come on, I wasn't done yet," I say, laughing as I move toward her. Julia flips her hair, curls bouncing down her back as she holds up her hands.

"I think this is it," she says, wide-eyed with anticipation. "It's about the right time."

"For what?" I ask.

Then the fountain, and I have my answer. The spray soaks me. I admit it; I yelp, almost toppling backward.

Julia laughs wildly, kicking the water, dancing around as the jets shoot a hundred feet into the air. Watching her in the softness of the coming dawn, I'm transfixed. I've never met anyone so free.

"What do you think?" she asks me, twirling around. I walk over and fold her into my arms. We kiss, and she tastes like coffee and sugar, the bite of tequila still on her breath.

She smells like the desert sun, feels soft and warm and perfectly alive in my arms. She's perfect. I look into her eyes, hold her against me.

"I think this feels good," I tell her.

"Like a happy ending?" she asks, slurring the words a little. She tries it again, this time articulating the sentence perfectly. I kiss her.

"I don't like when things end," I tell her, as we watch the fountain rise higher into the early morning sky, our arms around each other. "Beginnings, though. Those work great."

27

JULIA

"LAST ONE," I huff as I race up the stairs and into the condo, two lamps in my arms. One is my very precious vintage Minnie Mouse lamp in her polka dot dress, which I sure as hell wasn't leaving in Milwaukee. Nate comes up behind me, carrying a heavy cardboard box. His sleeves are rolled, his arms bunching with steely muscle as he takes the last couple of steps and kicks the front door shut behind him. Mmm. Steely muscle arms. Welcome home, indeed.

"Sure you don't have anything else?" he asks as he sets the box down and stretches. "A dead body you had stowed in the trunk?" He leans against the wall, his magnetic blue gaze growing even *more* magnetic with sarcasm. But it's one of the things I love about him.

One of many.

"I wanted to bring mine, but I was afraid it'd upset the *feng shui* of your house," I drawl, putting the lamps down. I still can't believe I'm living in any place as beautiful as a River North condo. We're up high, the twentieth floor, and the lights of downtown Chicago are sparkling along the river. The first few times I came here, I didn't really notice the view—Nate and I were pretty busy in the bedroom. But now that I'm an official resident, I have to admire it.

Nate's place is very modern alpha businessman sparse, with high end walnut furniture, soft sconce lighting, and sleek black couches. Minnie Mouse is going to have to find just the right corner. But she will.

"Now that we're done moving," Nate says, as he crosses over and takes me in his arms, "maybe we should celebrate." He kisses me, and it's ridiculous how after all these months, I still melt just a little. I wrap my arms around his neck as his hands ghost down my body, toying with the edge of my skirt.

"What'd you have in mind?" I whisper as he runs his fingers up my leg, my skin electric beneath his touch. Up and up and up—

"Champagne?" he asks, instantly stopping his progress and letting me go. Winking, he moves towards the kitchen. I huff.

"You tease!" I say, and he laughs. A moment later, he's got a bottle of Veuve Clicquet and two champagne flutes. Well, if we have to interrupt sexytimes, at least it's for a good reason. He pops the cork, pours, and we sit on his ultra-sleek couch in this ultra-sleek condo in an ultra-sleek Chicago neighborhood. When we first started seeing each other, I was afraid my being so un-sleek would clash with the lifestyle. But I think a little Minnie Mouse, sparkly purple, and Bangles music was what this place needed.

"Cheers," I say, as we clink glasses. I slip off my shoes

and curl up on the couch, my head against Nate's chest, his arm around me. We look out at the lights of the city and drink champagne. If there's any better homecoming than this, I don't want to know about it.

"You nervous?" Nate asks, kissing the top of my head. I was this morning, standing in my empty apartment with Shana in the car downstairs, waiting to drive me to my new life. I'm not now.

"Not at all. I even picked out my new writing spot," I say, pointing to a leather reclining chair by the window. "There. That's where I'm going to start my new series. High-profile lawyers battle it out by day and heat it up by night."

"Let me know if you need research," Nate says, as he starts kissing my neck. My toes curl. Oh, we'll need all the research. Oops, careful. I almost spill my champagne. I laugh as I put the glass on the table.

"You're a very manly muse," I tell him as I lean back into his embrace. My fingers trail along the chiseled line of his jaw. "You ever stop and think how crazy it is that all this happened? If Mike and Stacy had picked any other date or place to get married, if the conference had been delayed by a week, we'd have never met." I shrug as Nate's arms slide around me. "Maybe it was fate."

"I don't believe in fate," Nate says as he pulls me close and kisses me deeply. "But I do believe in luck," he murmurs against my mouth, his lips just grazing mine.

Everyone goes to Vegas hoping they'll get lucky. More often than not, they go home disappointed. Sometimes, though, just sometimes, you get lucky beyond your wildest dreams.

What happens then? You go all in.

THE END

Thanks for reading!

Want more laugh-out-loud romance reads? Keep scrolling for a sneak peek of the next book in the Lucky in Love series, BET ME. Available now!

Also read to the end for a look at my brand-new book. Cupids Anonymous is available to order now!

BET ME
Lucky in Love #2

What happens when your sex strike goes viral -- and suddenly every man in town has their eye on your *prize*?

All I wanted was little old-fashioned romance. After a parade of Tinder disasters who think chivalry is giving me a pearl necklace on the first date, I made a pledge: until guys step up their game, my goods are off the market.

But one bottle of chardonnay later, and my drunken rant has gone viral. I'm the most famous person NOT having sex since the Jonas Brothers put on their purity rings. A men's magazine has even put a bounty on my (ahem) maidenhead: fifty Gs to whoever makes me break the drought.

Be careful what you wish for...

Now my office looks like an explosion in a Hallmark factory, I've got guys lining up to sweep me off my feet - and the one man I want is most definitely off-limits. Jake Weston is a player through and through. He's also the only one who sees through the mayhem to the real me, but how can I trust he's not just out to claim the glory?

And how will I make it through the strike without scratching the itch - especially when that itch looks so damn good out of his suit?

The thrill of the chaste has never been so sexy in Lila Monroe's hilarious, hot new romantic read!

Available now!

1

LIZZIE

YOU KNOW what they say about a guy's hands. No, not that myth about dick size. I mean, that's what *they* might say, but I can confirm with an almost scientific certainty that hands don't lie. Guys with great hands—hands with fingers that can tease concertos out of a piano, or that have the light, sure touch necessary to make life-saving incisions with a scalpel—it's hands like that that will make you come your brains out. I mean, some girls are into arms, or abs, or the way a guy's happy trail leads down his stomach, but me? I'm all about the hands.

So there's a part of me that's both impressed and horrifyingly turned on as I watch Colin's near-surgical approach to tearing the chicken meat off one Super Sizzling Sweet Sauce-slathered chicken wing after another.

Be careful what you wish for.

"Sure you don't want any? It's two-for-one," Colin grins through a mouthful of chicken. "I've got a coupon and everything."

"Thanks, I'm good," I say weakly, watching those gorgeous, elegant hands smear barbecue sauce across his chin. So this is where a Sunday afternoon spent swiping right on cute dudes without bothering to read their profiles can land you come Monday evening.

I pick up my glass of warm chardonnay and try not to grimace. Not that he'd notice. I'm fighting to be heard in a packed sports bar just off of Times Square, where "the game" plays at an ear-splitting volume on an endless series of flat-screens, and the beer is served at such frigid temperatures that you almost forget that you're drinking something that would taste like piss if it happened to be warm.

"What in the fuck was that?" Colin yells suddenly, his hands flying up in tandem with every other dude in the bar—solo dudes who clearly didn't have the balls or the enterprising nature to combine Monday Night Football with a Tinder date.

"Sorry, sorry—I just can't believe this ref," he says, finally turning away from the screens. He shoots me a bashful smile, exposing a set of blindingly white teeth. "So what's your name again?" He downs his beer in one gulp and lets out an almighty belch.

Guys these days are so charming that I can hardly stand it.

Colin grabs another chicken wing like his life depends on it before pulling the meat from the bone and shoving it in his mouth. Before I can answer, he keeps talking, his mouth full of dead bird.

"So tell me more about this . . . what? Art shit, you said?"

His brow crinkles, as though the task of recalling the

few details I've ponied up about my life so far is about to give him a stroke.

"You're really into that stuff, huh? Old movies? My mom can't get enough of them. I don't know what she sees in those old dudes, though. Cary Grant? I mean, that stuff's from the dark ages. TV is where it's at. Have you seen *Ballers*? Now that's a great fucking show . . . Oh shit!" he yells out, jumping to his feet like he's been electrocuted, and his hip knocks into the table upending his entire glass of beer . . . in my lap.

Talk about a cold shower. I grab a pile of napkins off the table and start dabbing at my dress. This is definitely my cue to hightail it the hell out of here before something even worse happens. And let's be brutally honest: I'm pretty much lonely and horny enough that three more chardonnays might wind up with me being poked and prodded like another juicy wing by the end of the night.

"*Great* to meet you, Colin," I say sweetly, my cheeks hurting from the fake smile plastered across my face. I push my chair back from the table, the peanut shells littering the bar floor crunching beneath my heels. Colin may not have a romantic bone in his impressively-toned body, but there is no way in hell that I'm even going to consider hooking up with a guy who dares to blaspheme Cary Grant in my presence.

After all, a girl has to have standards.

A look of confusion flits across his face. "Wait . . . you're *leaving*? But the game's not over yet!"

Oh, it's definitely over. "Yeah, I'm sorry," I say, "but I have to get up early for work tomorrow. Let me know how it ends?"

"Sure," he says slowly. "And maybe we can do this

again sometime?" He cocks his head to the side and gives me an earnest smile, as if he has no idea that I can't wait to get the hell out of there. "I mean, this was fun, right?"

Oh sure. Like going to the dentist is fun. Like being trapped in a Turkish prison is fun . . .

I don't answer, turn around, and keep walking until I'm out the door. Miraculously, my Uber arrives almost right away and soon I'm slumped in the backseat, watching the twinkling lights of the Brooklyn Bridge flash by outside the window as we cross over the water from Manhattan.

The worst part is, I'd give that date a six. I mean, compared to the disasters I've been on, he's practically a knight in shining armor. Remembered my name? Check. All his own hair? Check. Didn't paw me in the coat-check line? Give this guy a medal and call it true love.

God, I've been dating in this town way too long.

At least New York will always make me feel better, even after the worst of bad dates—and I've definitely had my share lately. I try not to think about my track record until I'm home and can pour myself another glass of wine from an open bottle in the fridge and sink down into the couch, pulling my red heels off and throwing them across the room. It's not like they have far to go because my apartment is literally the size of a shoe box. A charming shoe box with exposed brick walls, windows overlooking Prospect Park, and a fire escape where I leave bowls of food for the neighbor's white Persian kitty (that I am slowly in the process of catnapping).

Everyone has to have a hobby, right?

But hey, it could be a lot worse. At least I don't have a roommate—or five.

Before I moved to Brooklyn from Toledo, Ohio, where I grew up, I pictured my first apartment as this charming, bohemian space where I'd store my Manolos in the oven a la Carrie Bradshaw and host glamorous parties like Audrey Hepburn in *Breakfast at Tiffany's*.

But Manolos are hard to come by on an assistant curator's salary, even at the Metropolitan Museum of Art. In fact, I've yet to have a single person over, much less an excuse to throw any kind of wild, Hepburn-esque soiree where people pass out face down on the floor while yelling "Timber!" Ever since the breakup with Todd, aka the man I thought was the love of my life, I've been too dejected and heartbroken to do much dating at all—until recently, that is.

And just look how *that's* turning out.

I reach over and grab my laptop off the floor and pull up Facebook, feeling better as I click to video message and the image of my sister, Jess, appears on the screen, looking none of her thirty-five years, with what looks like oatmeal smeared across one cheek.

Even though she still basically resembles a college student (Botox), she always seems completely stressed out, which is not exactly surprising considering the fact that she's raising two toddlers, Amelia, fourteen months (light of my life), and Jackson, three (devil's spawn), while trying to start her own internet business selling coffee mugs with the hashtags #Blessed and #Basic printed on them. When I asked her what she wanted for her birthday this year, she told me, "I want to check into a hotel for the night, order room service, and eat French fries while watching reality TV until I'm fucking comatose. Then I want to sleep for sixteen hours."

Motherhood is a joy.

"Lizzie, babe, what's up?" she asks.

"Oh my god," I say, reaching over and taking a sip of my wine, then pulling my legs beneath me so I can sit cross legged. "I just had the worst date *ever*."

Jess reaches one arm off screen, presumably to shove some goopy homemade concoction in Amelia's mouth, a smile twitching at the corner of her lips. "Ooh. Details. Gimme."

"You don't want to know."

"Please. I spent my day inventing elaborate fairytales to make my kids take their antibiotics. Remind me what adults even do, please."

"Watch a stranger devour hot wings in a crappy sports bar while completely ignoring their date?"

"Ouch," she winces, before her attention is yanked away. "Jackson! We don't strangle the dog!"

"Why are the kids still up?" I ask, fully aware that my sister hates to be off schedule. She runs her house like a military base—or a high-end prison.

"Don't ask," she sighs as she holds out a spoon to my niece. "Richard's working late and my night just went to shit. Amelia, open your mouth, sweetie," Jess coos before turning back to the screen with an exasperated look. "Why does she hate pureed parsnips," she mutters in exasperation, mostly to herself, "and why do you waste your time with these losers anyway?"

"What else am I supposed to do?" I moan. "Tinder is the only way anyone meets up these days, and these guys all *look* normal enough in their profile. Well, most of them, anyway," I say, backtracking quickly before she can call me out.

"Besides, I wasted my hot twenties on Todd, living in a crappy studio apartment, working that stupid sales job to make *his* dreams come true, and then he leaves me for his assistant! Now I'm THIRTY and stuck in this Tinder wasteland. I mean, the last three guys I hooked up with all stopped in the middle of sex to come on my tits! Not one, not two, but all *three!*" I despair. "Is romance totally dead, Jess? And more importantly, does my chest have a target painted on it or something?"

Jess bursts out laughing, still holding a goop-covered spoon in one hand. I can see Jackson running around behind her in their living room naked like some sort of crazed animal in need of a tranquilizer gun. "Lizzie! Not in front of the kids, okay?" she warns me, grinning. "And it's not like thirty is even old! I'm thirty-five, you know!"

"Yeah, but you're thirty-five with a husband and two kids living in a gorgeous house in Austin, Texas! I'm thirty with nothing waiting at home for me in the Naked City but this half-bottle of Two Buck Chuck." I gulp my wine like it's oxygen, aware that I'm rapidly crossing the line between tipsy and flat out drunk.

"I'm literally sobbing for you inside," she drawls. "I mean, it's Tinder! What were you expecting? That this guy was going to sweep you off your feet and you'd move into his penthouse in Tribeca and live happily ever after?"

I sigh, taking another sip of wine. Not expected. *Hoped* was more like it. I mean, is it so bad that I still believe there's a guy out there who might wine and dine me, and also fuck me like he's straight out of *Magic Mike XXL*? Who will send me flowers unexpectedly, leave little love notes in my purse, and bring home a bottle of prosecco just because?

The "told ya so" look on my sister's face answers the question for me with a resounding no. Clearly I'm not going to get much (read: any) sympathy from my own flesh and blood, so the only thing to do is clear—change the subject.

"So what's that on your *cheek*?" I ask mischievously, one eyebrow raised—a move that took me months to perfect in front of endless Joan Crawford movies. "Did Richard come home early and give you a *facial*?"

Richard's classically handsome with these waspy, blond-haired, all-American good looks, and is the sweetest guy ever. He's just . . . how can I put this? Not all that interesting? In fact, talking to him basically produces instant narcolepsy. I have no idea how Jess stays awake long enough to fuck him. She must recite the alphabet backwards or something.

"Oh my god," she says, literally recoiling in horror. "NO! That is so gross! We would . . . I would . . . never!" she stammers, her face the color of a summer tomato.

"Never is a mighty long time, Sis," I say with a wicked smile. "You should try it. What's the worst that could happen—you might actually have a good time?"

"You're completely depraved," she shoots back, practically sputtering now. "Richard and I have a *normal* sex life," she insists. "*Normal*. We would never do . . . any of *that*!"

See, what did I tell you? She's definitely reciting the alphabet when he fucks her. Or counting ceiling tiles. Besides, I love making my sister squirm. It's kind of like shooting fish in a barrel: a direct hit every time.

"Relax," I laugh. "You're probably getting more action

than me, even if it is on a schedule. Seven p.m. bath-time, seven-thirty p.m. bedtime stories," I tease. "Eight to eight-fifteen, conjugal intimacy."

"I hate you." Jess scowls, but she's laughing. "And I'll have you know, it's more like eight to eight-thirty."

"Go Richard!" I cheer. "Who'd have thought the man had it in him?"

AFTER WE HANG UP, I'm still not tired, even though I have to be up early, so I grab the remote and switch on the TV. When Jess and I were kids, before our parents finally split, I was dumped in front of the television practically every day after school while they had it out in the kitchen. As a result, TCM kind of became my best friend, and I still find it comforting to disappear into the fantasy land on screen: a world where the women are strong and sassy and well-dressed, and the men really know how to treat a lady.

A little champagne with dinner? Yes, please.

For once, I'm in luck—*An Affair to Remember* is on, lighting up the screen in glorious Technicolor. As I watch Cary Grant tenderly push back Deborah Kerr's flame-colored hair from her celestial face, I settle back into the cushions, pulling my feet underneath me. Now this is more like it. Waiting at the top of the Empire State Building for hours in the freezing cold for the woman you love, AND pining for her for years after she didn't show up? *That* was romance.

Coming on a lady's chest halfway through sex? *Please.*

I roll my eyes at the thought, draining my glass of wine and setting it down on the floor before curling up with my grandmother's purple knitted afghan.

Cary Grant would never pull that shit.

2

———

LIZZIE

WHEN I WALK into the museum the next morning, the sound of my boots clattering against the marble floors tells me I'm definitely hungover. Ouch. But even through my pounding headache, I still get the same kick as always, passing through the main hall with its gilded ceiling and ornate details. The Met is one of the greatest museums in the world, home to amazing works of art and culture, right on the edge of Central Park. I would come here all the time when I first moved to the city, just wandering the halls and taking in a new exhibition every other weekend. Todd always scoffed at it, saying I was obsessed with the past, but he never understood it wasn't about the artifacts, but the stories they told. A thousand different cultures over hundreds of years, all asking the same questions about life and love and our place in the world. The day I landed my assistant curator position, it felt like my life was finally back on track—I was doing something just for me, after spending so long following *his* plan.

But today, I barely give the grand staircase a second glance. Nope, I'm in emergency mode: heading straight for the basement in search of my next fix.

O coffee machine, where art thou?

A whistle pierces straight through my skull. "Someone had fun last night."

I groan. Our head of corporate PR, Bernard, is at the espresso machine, whipping up something perfect and espresso-adjacent. As usual, he's impeccably tailored in Italian cashmere and slacks. I hate him for being sober right now, but that doesn't mean I can't grovel to get what I need. "How much do you love me?" I say with a begging face.

He takes pity on me. "Enough to stop you making a fool of yourself. Here."

"Angel." I grab the tiny cup and gulp it down in one, then hold it out beseechingly.

He sighs. "Just one more, then I'm cutting you off. You've got a problem."

"Sure," I lie. "Whatever you say."

He sets the machine on again, then checks his phone. "Shit, I've got a donor call. Remember, just one more." He pauses. "And, umm, maybe do something about *that*." He gestures vaguely at my whole body before he heads off.

I don't blame him. My reflection in the silver espresso machine shows a pasty-faced ghoul staring back at me, so I reach into my purse for a tube of red lipstick, drawing it carefully across my lips. It's a trick I learned when I moved to the city—red lipstick forgives all sins. You know, like on mornings after I've consumed half a bottle of wine while lamenting the death of romance.

I pour another espresso, knowing I'll be back for more before noon, then navigate the narrow staircase that leads to my basement lair. The main museum itself is all airy hall-ways and massive exhibition rooms, but behind the scenes, it's a different story: a warren-like maze of back rooms and storage closets. When they first showed me to my office, a low-ceilinged box in the corner of the basement, I thought it was some kind of joke. Hazing for the newbie on her first day. But now that I've settled in, I kind of like it. The venti-lation pipes only rumble every half hour or so, and I deco-rated the walls with framed prints from classic Hollywood films like *Bringing Up Baby* and *The Philadelphia Story*, and my big bookcase is jammed with artifacts depicting love and romance through the ages. What can I say? I'm a nerd when it comes to ancient courtship rituals.

I'm just opening my laptop when Skye, my intern, comes bounding into the room. Well, "bounding" may be stretching it a bit since she's wearing a pair of wedge sandals so high I'm surprised she doesn't get a nosebleed just walking to work. With her long blond hair and curvy figure, she resembles a modern-day Veronica Lake, complete with that trademark swoosh of hair falling over one of her big green eyes.

I would hate her if she wasn't so naïve. It's hard to hold a grudge against a girl who thinks the guy who picked her up in a bar last night is a big-shot photogra-pher who, like, is totally going to make her a star now that she's done a private naked modeling shoot for him.

"Hey Skye," I yawn. "Did you get any memos through? I need to catch up before the staff meeting in case Morgan picks on me again."

"Never mind memos," she announces breathlessly. "Did you hear the news? Jake Weston is back!"

Crap.

Jake Weston. The name alone is enough to make my skin prickle with irritation. Jake is a freelance "finder," which means that he travels the world tracking down artifacts for museums, antique hounds, and private clients. If a basketball star wants a limited edition sneaker, Jake will find it. Front-row tickets to *Hamilton* on a moment's notice? Jake's your guy.

But the only interaction I've had with him so far has been over email, where "condescending" doesn't even begin to cover it. His favorite phrase is "Well, actually . . ." For some reason, every time I open his missives, I picture him as some tight-ass, fifty-year-old guy with rapidly thinning hair.

Apparently, he's been in Thailand recently, tracking down some rare statue of a golden monkey, and I guess he's finally back. Good thing, too, because as much as he annoys me, he's going to be indispensible in locating a few key pieces I need for the Golden Age of Hollywood exhibit I've finally managed to talk my boss into.

"Did you hear what I *said*?" Lizzie's voice cuts through the thoughts in my head, which is still pounding like crazy in spite of the coffee. "He's back!"

"I'll alert the media," I say dryly, closing my laptop. I'm clearly not going to get anything done with Skye blabbing at me a hundred miles an hour.

"The staff meeting is scheduled to start in five minutes," she says in a slightly disapproving tone, putting her hands on her hips and assuming the pose of a sexy-but-pissed-off third grade teacher. "Morgan asked me to make sure you were on your way since you were so late for last week's meeting."

"I was two minutes over!"

She shrugs. "Don't shoot the messenger. God, I'm tired," she yawns prettily, as I check email then grab my folder of notes for the meeting. "I worked at The Box till three last night. I'm trying out this new routine where I'm suspended from the ceiling and then lowered into a champagne glass filled with whipped cream. You would not *believe* how long it takes to get it all off," she says with a sigh, as if cleaning dessert off her body every night was absolute torture.

Skye moonlights as a burlesque dancer three nights a week at a club downtown. In her initial interview, she told me that either she wants to someday be a) a curator like me or b) Dita Von Teese. Good thing for her that she has plenty of time to decide.

"God, what I wouldn't give to be back in college," she moans. "I could sleep 'til noon every day and *still* make it to all of my classes. Those were the days, you know?" she says, her voice tinged with nostalgia that might be poignant if it wasn't so ridiculous.

"You only graduated last year, Skye," I say, resisting the temptation to roll my eyes. "And can you run and grab me another cup of coffee before the meeting? I had a bit of a late night myself." As soon as the words leave my mouth, I find myself stifling another yawn. Dammit, why are those things always contagious?

"Oooooh!" she squeals, the sound like a jackhammer in my brain. "Your life is so glamorous! Did you have a hot date?"

Let's see: I woke up still passed out on the couch in the

clothes I'd worn the night before, which stank of stale, cheap beer in the worst way possible. Not exactly glamorous. Or hot, for that matter.

"Hot? No. A date? Yes," I say, standing up and stretching my arms overhead and tugging at the big loopy bow at the neck of my blouse, which suddenly feels like it's strangling me.

"Don't worry," Skye says, "you'll *totally* meet someone. Probably when you least expect it. I mean, that's how I met Spencer." Her green eyes widen, and she moves closer, her expression serious as a government official's while revealing state secrets.

"I'd sworn off all guys for at least a *week*, and then in walks Spencer. He sat in the front row the first night I danced at The Box and picked up my rhinestone thong when I dropped it off the front of the stage during my 'Star Light, Star Bright' number, you know? The one with the American flag? Well, we've been together ever since," she says dreamily.

I blink at her uncomprehendingly. I'm not awake enough for this shit yet. Is ten a.m. too early for a drink? Because a little hair of the dog sounds pretty good right about now.

"That sounds . .   really romantic, Skye," I manage to choke out while gathering up my notes on the exhibition.

"Oh, it was," she says, snapping back to reality. "Most guys these days don't understand romance at all, but Spencer just *gets it*, you know? The other night, after I brought home Chinese food? He let me pick which fortune cookie I wanted before he did. He *knows* how much I love cookies!"

Oh my god, I think with a sigh. There's no hope for today's men. None at all.

Skye keeps chattering about Spencer's amazing romantic gestures (he puts the toilet seat down! Sometimes!) and I zone her out as we head upstairs for the staff meeting. My boss, Morgan, is already standing at the head of the conference room table. We're still a few minutes early, and the meeting hasn't even begun, but her expression makes it clear that she's five minutes past wanting to start.

"We're finally all here," she says, giving us a pointed look. "So let's begin."

I slide into a seat and realize too late Skye never got me that fourth cup of coffee. I'm going to have to face this one cold. And cold is the right word: our high priestess and overlord, Morgan, could put those ice queen femme fatales to shame. With her glossy dark hair, steely gaze, and eyebrows penciled into an expression of perpetual disapproval, she keeps our department running like a precision German automobile. From the 1940s.

"Bernard?" she demands sharply. "Updates?

We work through the upcoming calendar, touching on all the exhibits in progress. The Met prides itself on an eclectic program, and we have everything from Romanian folk art to a history of Black Pride protest photography. By the time she gets to my Hollywood show, I'm half asleep, but when I hear my name, I snap out of my hungover reverie and sit up straight.

"Lizzie is going to be making her debut as lead curator with a show this summer, which is, how should I say, a bit of a departure for the Met," Morgan says with a condescending smirk.

I swallow hard. I've been pushing the museum forever to curate an exhibition on the "Golden Age of Hollywood," and while the fact that Morgan finally said yes is a dream come true for me, I'm also painfully aware that curating the show is my biggest responsibility to date. I'm flying solo in the pilot's seat for the first time, and I can't fail if I ever want to move up the food chain at the museum.

"I can't wait to hear what she's planning," Morgan continues, icy, "but let's all congratulate her first on this milestone—which she hopefully won't make a mess out of."

Everyone giggles in a way that instantly makes me nervous. I stand up and smile to a round of polite applause, imagining lasers beaming down from above, burning through Morgan's herringbone pantsuit.

"Thanks, Morgan, for your confidence in me," I say, shooting her a smile so saccharine that I'm surprised she doesn't immediately get diabetes.

"I'm really excited about this opportunity," I continue. "I know Hollywood isn't our usual focus, but I think that now more than ever, in this age of digital media, where dating apps have largely taken over how people, meet, match, and break up with one another, romance has somehow fallen by the wayside. What I'm aiming to do with the Hollywood exhibition is to explore the movies' role in evolving romance narratives, showing how they interplay with more traditional courtship traditions, and built on them in the post-war era."

I look around for feedback, but everyone is checking their phones or zoned out, waiting to get the meeting over with.

"And as you may have heard," Morgan interrupts, "Jake Weston arrives this morning to begin working with Lizzie on acquisitions for the show."

Just like that, everyone perks up. The room fills with titters and low chatter, the air buzzing like a beehive that's just been kicked. I watch as two women who preside over the Egyptian wing bend their heads together, blushing and whispering furiously.

"So let's all be sure and give him your *full* cooperation with whatever he may need," Morgan continues. "Especially you, Lizzie." She gives me a condescending look. "Jake brings a wealth of experience, and I'm sure you can learn from him."

"Absolutely," I say through gritted teeth. "Now, as I was saying, about the exhibition—"

"No need, we get the picture." Morgan waves me down dismissively. "Next?"

I take a seat again, my blood already starting to boil. What is it with this Jake Weston guy, anyway? And why is he stealing my thunder for the most important moment of my career?

AFTER THE MEETING, I head back to my office and get to work. There are a million tiny details to plan for any exhibit, and right now, I'm still in the sourcing phase— trying to figure out what artifacts and pieces I can actually get in time, and how they can work together so the exhibition is more than just stuff sitting in a room. That's the real key to a great exhibit—everything needs to tell a story or show a different side to the theme, so that people walk away from it actually having learned something they never knew before, or have their perceptions changed.

I kick off my shoes and start sending emails, trying to track down not only a film print of *Casablanca* that I might be able to borrow for the show, but Humphrey Bogart's infamous trench coat and fedora to place in the exhibit. I'm deep in memorabilia dealers on the west coast when a sharp knock comes at my door.

"Wrong place," I call, without looking up. Nobody knocks around here, which must mean the mail kid is lost again. "Deliveries are at the end of the hall."

But the door swings open and a guy walks in. Not just any guy, but a drop-dead handsome man looking like he stepped out of a frame of a Bogart movie. He's got the leading-man chiseled jaw, and he's wearing a dark, slim-cut suit with the jacket stretching across his broad shoulders.

Hello, lover.

"Um, hi." I blink. Did this guy take a wrong turn in 1952 and wind up in my office? And can we please close the portal and never send him back?

I flush, suddenly wishing I'd at least had time to take a shower this morning. Deodorant spray covers many evils, but right now, I'd give anything to be fresh and bright and wafting the gentle aroma of a summer night's breeze. I clear my throat. "Can I help you?"

"I doubt it." He strides into the room like he owns it. Suddenly he's standing in front of my desk and holding out a hand for me to shake, his blue eyes sparkling. "I'm the one here to rescue your little exhibit."

"Little exhibit?" I repeat, tensing. I guess he brought his mid-century chauvinism with him through the slipstreams of time. "It's the major show of the summer season. And it doesn't need rescuing, by you or anyone else. Who are you, anyway?" I ask, gritting my teeth.

He looks at me like I should know already. "I'm Jake Weston," he says.

Wait, Jake?

Condescending Jake. "Well, actually" Jake. Bane-of-my-inbox-existence Jake?

Looks like *this*?

Damn. Talk about a waste of a gorgeous face.

"Hi," I answer, cooler now. He's got his hand outstretched to shake mine, so I reluctantly take it. "I'm Lizzie."

His grip is cool and firm, but the touch of his palm against mine makes something prickle in the back of my skull. I look at him again, harder. There's something familiar about him, a sneaking suspicion that tells me that somehow, somewhere, we've met before . . .

Holy shit!

It all comes flooding back to me. Whiskey and cold winter air, and the shrieks of New Year's Eve. I know this guy.

Intimately.

"Good to meet you," he says, his face friendly but impassive, his tone so nonchalant that he sounds almost bored. I stare at him incredulously, my mouth falling open slightly. Was my face so completely unmemorable? Or the rest of me, for that matter?

Oh my god, I can't fucking believe it. I look at him in disbelief, my throat suddenly tight and hot.

He doesn't even remember me.

He doesn't remember the fact that the last time I saw

the man standing in front of me and calling himself Jake Weston, he was passing out unconscious. . .

With his face buried between my legs.

TO BE CONTINUED...
Jake and Lizzie's story is just getting started. #2 in the Lucky in Love series, BET ME, is available now - CLICK HERE to read!!

Cupids Anonymous
A Romantic Comedy

Readers around the world are raving over USA Today bestselling author Lila Monroe's hilarious romantic comedies. Now fall in love with her brand new sizzling standalone - perfect for fans of Sophie Kinsella and Christina Lauren!

Poppy Hathaway is a professional Cyrano - minus the honking great nose. Need a love note, raunchy sext, or apology letter so epic that your other half will forget you hesitated a beat too long when you asked, 'does this make me look fat?'? She's got you covered. But when her most frequent client, the annoyingly charming (or is that charmingly annoying?) Dylan Calloway comes to her with an unconventional new job, Poppy discovers that three little words can add up to one big complication.

Because Dylan doesn't want help seducing another swimsuit model (for once in his life). He wants Poppy's help breaking up his sister from her dirtbag gold-digging boyfriend - and he's prepared to make it worth her while. Throw in a summer Catskills trip that's equal parts 'Dirty Dancing' and dirty-talking, and this Cupid is soon out of her depth - and head over heels with the last man she expected. But can she find the right words when it comes to her own heart? Or will this happily ever end in disaster?

Find out in the sparkling new romantic comedy from Lila Monroe!

Cupids Anonymous is available to order now!

1

POPPY

I FOUND my calling in life when I was twelve years old.

My younger brother, Noah, had a crush on a girl in school, but being a boy – and a gross, stinky one at that – his idea of romance was to shoot spitballs at her, and chase her around the playground. Enter me. Two whole years older, eons wiser, and equipped with a romantic spirit and a love of cheesy rom-coms. I wrote him a cute note to pass to her in class, inviting her to split a pack of cookies at break. What girl could turn down a free snack? Nobody worth dating, as far as I'm concerned.

And, sure, she turned out to have a peanut allergy, and wound up being rushed to the E.R, but for those three glorious minutes before she started choking, my brother had found love. And I had found my future career. Because everyone knows, true love needs a little help sometimes. The right words to say exactly what's on our minds.

Or rather, the romantic version, minus the peach emojis and dick-pics.

That's where I come in. Your own personal Cyrano –
just without the honking great nose. I'll craft you the
perfect love note, compose a dirty email to get your paramour panting, and write the most epic apology, it'll make
your other half forget that you hesitated a beat too long
when they asked, 'Does this make me look fat?'

Maybe I'm a big softie at heart, but I love being able to
give romance a helping hand. There's no task too big
when it comes to my clients, no challenge too great...

Which is why I'm halfway up a tree in Central Park,
feeding lines through a tiny microphone to the man
proposing to his girlfriend just below.

"Since the moment I laid eyes on you in the virtual
reality game, I knew, you were the one I wanted to quest
with me – in real life."

Henry dutifully repeats every word, in front of a small
circle of family and friends. I tried to talk him out of that
part – public proposals seem like a recipe for massive
humiliation – but he insisted. But now, I'm the one at risk
of embarrassing myself, if I can't keep hidden up in this
tree for another page of heartfelt devotion.

The tree branch lets out an ominous creak.

Oh crap. I lean forwards, trying to spread my weight –
and not miss my place in the proposal.

"And as Leia said to Hans, I've always hated watching
you leave..." I whisper, reading off my cellphone screen.
Henry says the line, and everyone in the crowd breathes a
swoony, 'ahhh'. His girlfriend is already crying. Happy,
oh-my-god tears, and not 'get me out of here' sobs.

I hope.

The branch creaks again, and I cling on for dear life, as
Henry makes it through the rest of the proposal.

"So, Kelly, will you make me the happiest man in the galaxy, and agree to be my wife?"

There's a pause, and I grip on tighter, sending up a silent prayer. Please let her say 'yes', and go celebrate someplace else, before this proposal literally comes crashing down to earth.

"Yes! I will! Yes!" the girlfriend sobs, and I let out a huge sigh of relief.

Way to go Henry!

The group cheers, and the happy couple embraces, and even though I've got ants crawling over me, I'm thrilled for the two of them. I've been a part of this relationship from the beginning, since Henry hired me to help write his dating profile, and I'm pretty sure I'll be the one composing anniversary cards until the pair are old and grey.

Like I said, some people just have a little trouble expressing themselves. And if I can help them tell their loved ones how they feel, well, it's all in a day's work.

I will, however, be billing him for my laundry, because I don't even want to know what's smeared all over my jeans by now. I wait until the crowd disperses, then set about gingerly inching my way back off the branch.

It groans in protest.

"Hey," I mutter ruefully. "I only had two portions of dumplings last night. And I totally drank a diet soda!"

I wriggle back and awkwardly turn to hug the trunk. Just a little further—

CRACK. The branch gives way, and my hands slip. I flail wildly, but it's already too late: I'm slip-sliding down the trunk, hitting what feels like every stump and splinter on the way as I bounce my way to the ground.

OOF.

I groan, laying on the dirt in a shower of leaves and twigs.

"I should have guessed this proposal was your handiwork."

I look up to find six foot two of lean muscle, blue eyes, and irritatingly-charming sarcasm. Dylan Calloway. Another client of mine – and the bane of my existence.

"How could you tell?" I ask, sitting up with a wince.

"Your undeniable literary style," Dylan replies. He offers me a hand, and hauls me to my feet again. "Plus, the fact that Henry was way too calm," he adds. "The man sweat through a three-piece suit giving a toast at his parent's anniversary dinner. The fact he made it through a single line without stuttering was a major giveaway you were somewhere around here, pulling the strings."

"No strings!" I protest. "Henry wrote every word. I just… polished, that's all."

"Sure you did." Dylan grins. "The same way Rodin just polished those lumps of marble into statues."

I blink. "What's that? A compliment?" I hold my hand to my ear, teasing.

Dylan smirks. "You know you're good. I wouldn't hire anyone but the best."

"There *is* nobody else," I remind him. The market for a professional Cyrano is slim-to-none. Which is why I have to go the extra mile for my clients.

Or up the extra tree.

"Nice touch, with the Star Wars quote, by the way," Dylan remarks, as we stroll out of the wooded area. He's wearing his trademark black jeans and a white button-down, looking annoyingly handsome in the bright summer sun. With his classic Ray-Bans and unruly dark hair, he's every inch the 'hot rich guy you know is destined to blow you off but you can't help fantasizing about him all the same'.

Or maybe I just watched too many John Hughes movies at an impressionable age?

Either way, I know way too much about Dylan to ever entertain the idea of dating him. Like how he runs through women the way I run through Sephora skincare samples. Or the fact that as a mere mortal – and not, say, an international swimsuit model-slash-actress-slash human rights lawyer – I probably don't even register as a prospect to him.

Sure enough, we're just turning onto the path when a gorgeous brunette woman stalks towards us, looking annoyed. "Where have you been?" she demands, looking annoyed.

I say 'woman', but let's face it, she's so beautiful, she probably deserves another scientific classification, because I'd be surprised if we shared even half our DNA. Her hair is long and glossy, her face is all eyes and cheek-bones, and there isn't just a thigh-gap between those tanned legs in her teeny-tiny cut-offs, there's the whole Grand Canyon.

"Gigi, I've been right here," Dylan protests.

Gigi?

I try not to smile. Of course. His latest paramour. She loves expensive roses, Adele songs, and inspirational quotes. Which I know because Dylan has had me composing love notes for her all week. And looking at her now, I can see why.

"You said to meet you by the trees." The exquisite

beauty known as Gigi pouts. "Do you know how many trees there are in Central Park?"

"I'm sorry, baby." Dylan turns on the charm, flashing her a mega-watt smile. "Let's go get you a drink."

But Gigi isn't convinced.

"You're always doing this," she says. "I blew off a sample sale to come meet you, but you don't even care. You're over here, flirting with—" she looks at me, frowning.

"Nobody." I answer quickly. "Really."

"She's just a friend," Dylan insists. "Come on, babe, you can't imagine I'd have eyes for anyone except you."

And Sophie. And Lara. And the girl from the coffee shop Dylan wanted to woo with Shakespeare quotes and roses just last week. But maybe Gigi is smarter than I thought, because she isn't buying his Romeo act anymore.

"No! This isn't working. You need to figure out what you need," Gigi gives a tearful sniff. "Before you lose the best thing that ever happened to you."

She turns on her (stacked, five-inch platform) heels, and sashays away.

"Well, that went well."

I turn. Dylan is looking strangely cheerful for a man who just got dumped. "You don't mind?" I ask, surprised.

"Mind what? She'll come around." He shrugs. "That's what I have you for. I'll take one of your apology packages. A sincere note, a couple of poems... She'll be back in my arms by the weekend."

I roll my eyes. "You're incorrigible."

"That's why I'm your favorite client." Dylan grins.

"My most frequent client," I correct him. And it's true.

Dylan has been keeping the lights on with his commissions these past months.

His many, many commissions.

From flirty notes tucked inside massive bouquets, charming women into dates with him, to heart-felt apology notes when he inevitably lets them down, Dylan Calloway is a one-man seduction machine.

And I'm the voice behind the pen, helping it happen.

I sigh, strolling towards the exit. "Remind me again why I'm your accomplice in these crimes against true love?"

"Because you believe that even I deserve a chance to find my soulmate?" Dylan offers, teasing.

"Nope, try again."

"Then it must be the cold hard cash." Dylan pats me on the shoulder. "Oh, before I forget, I might have another job for you."

"Another one?" I exclaim. "Seriously, where do you find the time? I can't even get a moment to go take in my dry-cleaning, let alone juggle four different dates."

"It's an art," Dylan agrees. "What can I say? I'm an excellent multi-tasker."

"Don't you ever get tired of it?" I ask, with equal parts admiration and disdain. "Or say the wrong name, and mix them up?"

"That's a rookie mistake," he laughs. "You need to switch to general endearments. Babe, honey, sugar-lips. That way, you never get it wrong. Especially not in the… *heat* of the moment."

He winks. Now he's just messing with me.

"Sure thing, sugar-lips," I reply, shaking my head with a smile. "So, who's the unlucky target this time?"

"I'm still figuring that part out," he replies, mysterious. "I'll swing by the office this week to discuss. For now, just focus on getting me back in Gigi's good graces."

"Lucky me."

"Chin up." He grins. "This will be easy. Just use the line from that movie again."

"*I'm just a man, standing in front of a woman?*" I suggest.

"That's the one. They always go crazy for it."

"Hugh Grant has a lot to answer for." I sigh.

And so do I.

TO BE CONTINUED...

Poppy and Dylan's hilarious story is just getting started.

Cupids Anonymous is available to order now!

ABOUT THE AUTHOR

Combining her love of writing, sex and well-fitted suits, Lila Monroe wrote her first serial, The Billionaire Bargain, in 2015. She weaves sex, humor and romance into tales about hard-headed men and the strong and sassy women who try to tame... love... tame them. Her books are extensions of her own fantasy life and take readers from the boardroom to the Berkshire Mountains, with keen character development, unique plot lines, and fanciful romance.

www.lilamonroebooks.com
lila@lilamonroebooks.com